IT'S NOT ABOUT THE DOG

STORIES

BY

SUSAN TAYLOR CHEHAK

FOREVERLAND PRESS
Silverthorne, Colorado
www.foreverlandpress.com

ISBN: 978-0-9960408-7-7

Cover Design by www.ebooklaunch.com

For Jack Leggett, who first believed in me
1917-2015

IT'S NOT ABOUT
THE DOG

My younger sister Daisy lives in New York City, and big whoop. You can tell she thinks that fact makes her special, like she believes she's risking her life just by getting up in the morning every day. She's an actress, but nobody that I know has ever heard of her.

"How can you stand to live out here in the middle of nowhere, Iris?" she asks, as if this wasn't at one time her hometown too. She waits, but I am not going to play. She studies me. "Oh, I get it," she says. "You guys think you're safe."

She has started right in with it, the minute she's off the plane. The smell, the heat, the double-bacon-cheeseburger-with-fries fat family pulling their bags off the belt at baggage claim, the Bush/Cheney sticker on the bumper of a mud-spattered pickup, the fish emblem on the broad backside of a new minivan, the flags in the yards, and the yellow ribbons on the trees.

"God, how much do I hate this fucking place," she says, and then smiles at me. "No offense."

When we get in the car Gene makes my sister pay him five dollars before he'll roll up the windows and turn on the air for her, and then he calls her a hypocrite for asking him to waste the gas.

The billboard standing in a cornfield: "God is Pro Life, Are You?" Daisy muttering, "Life is choice, you freaks."

Gene's hand moves to my knee and stays there.

Of course, Daisy is free to believe whatever she wants to believe, and she can say what she wants to say, then go on and tell the whole world all about it too—put it up on a billboard by the highway, if that's what makes her happy—but the fact is, Gene and I have made a real good life for ourselves together here, and I don't know why we should be expected to feel guilty for that. Or less than adequate or stunted or stupid or weak or selfish or dishonest or criminal, or whatever it is that my sister wants to try to make me feel about myself.

She stands on the front porch, studying the street while Gene gets her bags out of the car. We moved into the Paradise tract two months ago; this is the first she's seen of it. Everything's brand new, even the trees. The community is in such high demand; she has no idea how lucky we were to get in.

"Jesus, Iris," she says, "this place looks like a movie set." At first, it's hard to tell whether she means this as a compliment or not. "It's like it isn't real." Most likely not, and I can feel my face heating up, but Gene's wink reminds me not to be so sensitive. He shoulders past her into the house, flashing his teeth. "You want real, Daisy. I'll show you real."

When she laughs, it's in a way that gives out more breath than sound. Her lipstick shines. "Dream on, big boy," she says, because she is aware of my husband's condition. I know now that I never should have confided in her, but I was drunk that night on the phone, and I was feeling sorry for myself, and who else do I have to talk to about something like that? Not Mom. Not Rose. "Get a vibrator, Iris," she told me then. "You have some lubricant. Get him some Viagra."

Rose has been waiting for us in the kitchen. She's at the table working on her squares, and the dog sits at her feet, panting. Square after square my big sister knits from scraps of yarn—she doesn't care what color or what kind—and then she pieces them together into blankets for the needy. Sometimes she gets fancy with the stitches, but mostly she just goes back and forth and they all come out close enough to the same. She once tried to get me and Daisy to join her in this endeavor, but Daisy didn't have the time or the inclination, and I don't have the patience or the skill. The finished blankets come out a little uneven and mixed up, but they're plenty warm and that's all that counts.

If Daisy is the pretty one and I am the smart one, then Rose is the large one who looks the most like our mother, as if something has rubbed off on her because it wasn't until she was well into her thirties that she had a home of her own, and even then only a block-and-a-half away. She blames her weight on the time when her appendix burst and she almost died, which was more than twenty years ago now, but never mind. Rose says that the antibiotics they gave her during that time changed her metabolism and that's why at thirteen years old she grew out of being a small pixie girl with short bangs and a long braid down her back to become this slow-moving, slow-thinking woman that she is now—dressed in big shorts and a man's shirt, with a helmet of graying hair, cropped short to save herself the bother of having to do anything much to take care of it.

Gene fixes Daisy a vodka tonic. Greasing the gears, I know, because he likes to get her talking. Waving her arms around and such, working up a sweat. He tells her she's a beautiful woman as it is, but she's even prettier when she's mad, which only makes her madder to hear it said, which only makes her prettier, and so on. She wears a stack of gold and silver bracelets on her left wrist, and she can't take them off because they've been soldered into circumferences that are smaller than the width of her hand. This is to remind her of her mortality, she says. She describes it as an act of self-love. Gene and I both are watching her breasts bounce around inside her sheer white blouse—something delicate and expensive—and Daisy is aware of this too, it seems. She gets fidgety, lifting her shoulders and pulling her hair up off the back of her neck to cool herself down. This is Iowa and it's summertime, humid and hot as ever.

Gene is at the counter cutting up limes while Daisy fans her face and tells us about the melting icecaps and receding glaciers.

Rose is oblivious of all that. She keeps to herself mostly anyway, but for sure, she won't join in a conversation that might have turned to politics. It's all just talk to her, and she considers having an opinion to be a waste of time. You can't just watch the news and get mad about this or that or whatever and then imagine that means you have some part in what goes on. It isn't enough to just think and talk, she says, you also have to do.

"Do what?" Daisy asks. "Knit blankets?"

But Rose will not be baited. You cannot get to Rose. She is as placid as a puddle. Medicated, is my guess.

Gene finds a reason to squeeze around Daisy, reaching for a bowl to fill with cocktail nuts. His eyes follow her as she moves out of his way, and then they turn to me.

Daisy ought to know that we are not greedy people, Gene and I. We have always had just what we need and not so very much more. I have made it a point to take care of myself, and so my health is good, and I am a burden to no one. I recycle, even if my husband doesn't. I don't drive one of those big gas-guzzlers — my Saturn gets me wherever I have to go, which is never very far. I keep our thermostat low when it's cold and high when it's hot. I remember to turn off the lights when there's nobody in the room, and I make it a point to run my appliances on the off-peak hours when I can. If we have a nice house, that's because together Gene and I do whatever needs to be done to keep it clean and in good repair. We pick up after ourselves, we do our own chores, and we don't have to hire foreigners to come in and help us out with the dirty work. The place is all paid for. We have some good investments. We try to pay with cash, we don't like to use credit, and we do not live in debt.

My whole life, I have done my best to be responsible. Accountable. Reliable. Sensible. Strong. I have always tried to do my part.

I would like for Daisy to understand: this is our world. It's peaceful. It's quiet, it's clean, and it's neighborly. We care about each other here. We look after our own. And if it comes to it, we are willing to do whatever it takes to protect ourselves against those people who hate us for being who we are and for having what we have. We have gates, we have walls, and the security car passes by our house regularly, day and night.

Daisy settles in at the table across from Rose. "So tell me what happened."

Rose smiles. "Well, I'm just fine Daisy. Thanks for asking. It's good to see you too."

"I'm sorry. This is hard for me."

"It's hard for all of us."

Daisy nods. Her eyes fill with tears.

Rose watches her swipe at them with the back of her hand. "She's anxious to see you."

Our mother is in the hospital again; that's why

Daisy is here. Last time it was pneumonia, and it was something about her lower intestine the time before that. Over the last couple of years, these incidents have become so common as to seem routine, and we follow the patterns of our own behavior in such circumstances as if they've all been laid out for us already.

This time it's a fall. She missed the bottom step into the back yard, and was down on the ground for a couple of hours before Rose found her, sunburned and delirious, with her pelvis cracked and her left leg broken in two places.

Daisy asks, "How's she doing?"

Rose says, "Oh, she'll be all right, I guess. She's looking forward to seeing you."

"First thing in the morning."

"She can't stop apologizing."

"For what?"

"For everything. For being a nuisance. For being old. For not being able to take care of herself. For making it so you have to interrupt your busy life and spend all that money to come back here because of her."

"That's crazy." She's digging in her purse for a cigarette, although she must know that she'll have to go outside to smoke it.

Through this, Rose has not stopped knitting. Her needles flare in the lenses of her glasses. "You know how she is. She even blames herself for falling down. Clumsy. Bad shoes. Should have had her glasses on. That sort of thing. She doesn't want to be a bother to anybody."

"What she should have had is a cell phone, or one of those emergency medical beepers. Jesus, what if it had rained?"

Rose just shakes her head.

"Where were you?" Daisy wants to know. "Where the hell was Bear?"

He hears his name and stands up, wagging his tail and rolling his eyes, showing their whites. While Mom was out there on the ground, Bear was inside the house throwing himself against the door and chewing through the linoleum in the kitchen. He yelps when Daisy pushes him away.

Outside on the back deck, Gene has fired up the grill, and I've got the citronella candles lit to keep the bugs at bay. The day has started rolling over into night, the trees that separate our lot from the one behind us are thickening into their own shadows, and the fireflies have started to come out. Rose is down on the lawn playing fetch with Bear. She makes him wait, winds him up, watches him hop and turn, yelping with impatience, before she lets go, and then he flies, crashing into the bushes and skidding back out again, grinning around the tennis ball held softly in his teeth. Daisy eyes the hamburgers I've brought out and shakes her head.

"I don't eat meat, Iris," she says.

"Since when?" I ask.

"And neither should you," she adds.

Gene asks, "Why not?"

She counts the reasons off on her fingers while Gene lays the patties out on the hot grill. Animal suffering, rainforest destruction, energy consumption, topsoil depletion, world hunger, clean water, clean air, mental well being, and personal health.

"In that order?" When Gene smiles the skin around his mouth cracks and folds in on itself, and his face goes all to pieces.

Daisy ignores him, and turns to me. "Did you know that if we reduced our consumption of meat by only ten per cent, we could save enough grain to feed the sixty million people on the planet who die of hunger every year? Think about that, Iris, next time you're at the store. If it weren't for our government subsidies, that burger there would have cost you thirty-five dollars a pound."

"You're in farm country here, Daisy," I tell her. "Cows and pigs and corn are what we do."

I lean in closer to my husband and feel the heat surging up from the grill. When I reach for the meat platter his fist moves to the small of my back, and I let him run his thumb along the bumps of my spine, twanging at me like stretched string. He nods toward Daisy's empty glass. "How about getting your sister another drink, Iris."

She rattles the ice and begs, "Yes, pretty please? I'll be good, I promise."

When I come back outside, Gene is holding a candle and Daisy is bending toward him to light her cigarette from its flame. She throws her head back on the exhale, exposing her throat. She props an elbow on the deck rail, fiddling with the cigarette pack and looking over her shoulder to eye Rose and Bear still at their game down in the yard.

"So you smoke, but you don't eat meat?" I ask.

"I'm not perfect," she says, as she takes the glass from me. "No matter what anybody says."

Gene laughs at this.

Daisy waves her cigarette at him. "It's nice to hear you laugh. You should do that more often." She turns to me. "You know what we need a little less of in this world, Iris?"

I shake my head. "What's that?"

"Suffering. We need less suffering."

I nod. "Okay."

"Less suffering and more love."

I wait.

"And you know how we get more love?" She

smiles and opens her arms as if she would embrace us all. "Empathy. We get it with empathy." She lets this sink in, then goes on, "I know this is true because that is what I do." The bracelets skitter and chime with each sweep of her hand. "Acting, you see."

Gene laughs again, but this time she ignores him. She is talking to me now; she is explaining.

"My job " She tosses her hair. " My job is to be whoever they tell me to be, and to be any good at that I have to make it real. Even if it isn't me, even if I don't believe what the character believes, I have to become her anyway." She leans closer. "I have to erase myself, all right?"

I nod.

"And to do that I have to find in myself whatever it is about her that is also in me." She peers at me to check that I'm paying attention. "Because what happens is, after a while you realize…" She pulls back. "You realize that we are really all the same." She looks at Gene; his eyes flick to me. She taps her ashes over the rail. "We all have the same feelings and thoughts and dreams and everything, when you come down to it. And we all want the same things." She ticks them off on her fingers. "Food, clothing, shelter. That's it!" She pauses, then: "Okay, and entertainment. Something to keep our minds busy. I'll grant you that."

We wait. She looks at me again.

"Okay, and safety, too. We want to be safe. We want our kids to be safe. We want all our loved ones to be safe." She nods, agreeing with herself. "But really, we should want everybody to be safe, and if we realized that we are all the same, we would. If we could just get it that there is no difference between you, Iris, and some woman in Palestine who is trying to hold on to her little patch of dirt or sand or whatever it is that they have over there… Well, if we realized that then there would be no war. No war! You know what I mean, right?" Now she's talking to Gene. "We all just want to be able to go about our business, whatever our business is. That's all. Everybody wants that. Every single person. You, me, everybody. Nobody wants to die."

Gene nods. He flips the burgers, one by one.

"Not even the animals, Iris. Not even the cows and pigs." She takes a swallow of her drink, grits her teeth. "Not even me," she says, then adds, "anymore."

She knows that I know what's under the bracelets. I start to respond, but she cuts me off.

"Don't bother." She waves me away. "I know what you're going to say."

Gene sniffs at this. "Well, hell Daisy, we're all ears," he says. "Show us some of that empathy you've got. Erase yourself, like you said."

My sister smiles. Ever since she was little, she has loved to perform. She takes one last drag and then stubs her cigarette out. She pulls her hair back from her face and wraps it into a knot. Rubs the lipstick off her mouth with the back of her hand. Puts her fists on her hips, plants her feet. Lifts her chin, scowls hard. "We're all going to die," she says. She coughs, suppresses a smile. She rolls her shoulders, stretches her neck, and takes a deep breath. "There's nothing I can do." She coughs again, clears her throat, and shakes her head.

Gene's hand is on my arm. His fingers squeeze. He is holding me in place.

She has folded her hands together now. "I don't understand why they have to hate us so much," she whines. "It's not MY fault. I never did anything to anybody." She looks at me and raises her eyebrows, questioning, then pulls back and goes on, reciting: "They're always picking on me. I'm not as smart as they are. It's not fair." She's getting stronger. She pounds her fist into her palm. "They have NO right to treat me like that. They are SAVAGES! They aren't HUMAN! It isn't ME! I didn't do ANYTHING! There's something wrong with THEM! They're CRAZY!"

She's no longer herself. She has become me. She leans close, whispers: "Somebody has to stop them or else they're going to wreck everything. That's what they want. We have to destroy them before they can destroy us." She turns away. We wait. Gene's grip on my arm has tightened and it's painful, but before I can pull away from him, Daisy whirls around and is upon us, on her toes and looming. Her voice cracks, spills words: "We'll hunt them down we'll never stop we'll smoke them out we'll make them bleed We'll catch them we'll cut them we'll hang them we'll kill them. They will be OBLITERATED!" She opens her arms, throws back her head, thrusts out her hips, bends her knees, swings her pelvis, and shakes her belly and her breasts. Her whole body rises like a wave, bearing down on us as she bellows: "Ka-a-a-a. BOOM!"

I cling to Gene and close my eyes, but when I open them again it's only Daisy standing there, diminished, panting and flushed. Her blouse clings to her skin. She shakes her hair loose - it's matted, soaked. She fingers a cigarette from the pack, and her hands tremble as she lights it. She sinks onto the chaise. She puts her head back, shuts her eyes, and lets her arms hang loosely at her sides. She is a monster made of rags.

Gene brings his hands together, and he heavily applauds. "Was that as good for us as it was for you?" he asks.

Her smile is weak, so maybe so.

While down in the yard, Rose's throw is powerful, and Bear's passion for it is unrelenting.

"It's called Canine Separation Anxiety," Rose says. Daisy frowns. She's reapplied her lipstick, and it gleams. "Maybe he should see a psychiatrist."

Gene laughs at this. "Jesus." He snaps his fingers. Bear lifts his head. Alert, he watches Gene.

Rose goes on, "He doesn't like to be alone."

Daisy takes a last bite of salad and then pushes her plate away. "Yeah, well, who does?" She raises her wineglass to the light, eyes it, and flashes a smile at me. She waggles a finger at the dog, jangling the rings around her wrist. "I'm one hundred per cent with you on that one, Bear."

Rose smoothes her napkin over her empty plate. "It's not just what he did to the kitchen, Daisy. He destroyed one of the good chairs, too. He's chewed the wood on the back door right down to the glass. He ripped up the floor in the bathroom and dug a hole in the mattress on her bed. He's gone into her closet and shredded all her shoes. The whole house is a mess, and it's going to cost a lot of money to have it repaired."

Daisy puts her glass down, serious now. "So what are you going to do?"

Gene says, "Put him down."

"You can't put him down."

Rose says it again, slowly, "He can't be left alone."

"No. Mom'll go nuts. She won't allow it."

And then it's my turn. "You know she isn't going home this time, don't you Daisy?"

Rose backs me up. "Mom can't be left alone anymore either."

Daisy lets this sink in. "Where will she go?"

"We'll have to find a place for her."

"A home," I say. "Managed care. There are lots of them around. Some are very nice."

Daisy shakes her head.

"You want to take the dog back to New York with you, Daisy?" I ask.

"You know I can't do that."

"All right then," Rose says, "do you want to move here and take care of both of them together?"

That shuts her up, just as we knew it would.

Once the table is cleared, and the dishes are done and put away, Gene and I will find my sisters curled together on the sofa in the darkened living room. Daisy's eyes are closed; her head rests on Rose's shoulder; and she abides in the cradle of her older sister's arms. Bear lifts his head, his tail thumps the floor, and we're hushed by Rose's finger to her lips.

I follow my husband up the stairs to our bedroom at the top. This is our life together; this is our routine. We undress separately and silently, in the dark. My nightgown is hanging on the back of the closet door. I put it on, then take it off again. In the bathroom, I brush my teeth and wash my face and avoid the look I get from my reflection.

I slide into my bed beside Gene. The sheets are cool, his skin is warm. He reaches behind me, draws me in, spreads my body flat against his. He knees apart my thighs, he cups me in his palm, and he opens me with his hands. His weight shifts, he hovers then sinks, and I fold myself around him, hold him there, sturdy and strong. We stay still; we wait; we don't move. Clasped together, skin to skin, we have become one body and one being. The world cracks apart, the abyss opens, we fall into the void and are gone.

Beyond the yard lights, the night is black, the wall is high, the gate is locked, the security car prowls, and this is how we will keep ourselves safe, from any and all harm.

WITNESS

If you were above it all somehow, at a window, say, and high enough over the street to be able to see what happened, but not so far that the details would be blurred. Many floors, or maybe just a few. Six, say. If you were in a room on the sixth floor of a ten-story hotel and you were at the window, having a smoke, say. In a non-smoking room. With your morning coffee and the newspaper waiting. The bed still warm. The sheets a mess. Your hair a mess too. His shirt on your back. No, not his shirt, because he was already gone by then; that's why you were at the window, not for the smoke, you don't smoke, not anymore, not since you watched your mother gasp her last.

You were at the window so you could watch him go. You were wondering if he might look up and see you there. He was at the crosswalk; he was waiting for the light, and it was early by some standards. By your standards. The street was full of cars, and the sidewalk was full of people, considering that this was not a big city. This was not New York, and downtown hadn't been the same since the flood three years ago that rose up to the middle of the first floor of the buildings around here and left a fish in the lobby of the hotel and ruined the public library, washed away police records and evidence rooms, made a mess of the little houses in the pocket closest to the river, where you used to live, where you grew up.

Still, this was his hometown, and he kept his downtown office, determined to move back in and get back to normal as soon as possible. He had the place cleaned up and set to rights in record time. Hardly missed a day of work, because he loved his job, at least the concept of it if not the actual content. Which was insurance. And there's an irony in that, I know.

So he was at the crosswalk waiting for the light, and maybe you were disappointed that he didn't happen to look up to see you watching, to see you admiring him—the square of his shoulders, that open circle of bare scalp at the back of his head, gleaming because it was warm and he was hatless. Someone next to him—a younger man he might have known—said something to him, and he replied, and the light changed, and he began to cross toward those who had begun to cross toward him from the other side.

A split second, as you described it for us. Only one step, two at the most. When from out of nowhere, someone else said—because isn't that what they always say?—from out of nowhere, suddenly, there was a car. Except it wasn't from out of nowhere at all, it was from out of somewhere; it was from out of the far side of the crosswalk. And it wasn't just a car, it was also a driver, a kid at the wheel, a young man who had miscalculated. He was not drunk. He was not high. He was in a hurry and he didn't think. He was impatient, so he slipped around into the right turn lane, and he gunned it, misjudging by only a fraction of a second how much time he had, by only a few feet how much space, just that much but enough that rather than fly through and on, instead he slammed into the first pedestrian off the curb.

You were at the window, which was closed, so you didn't hear the sound except in your head—a bang that shook you just as he was hit and thrown up off his feet and over the hood, where he hovered for a moment as the car and its driver passed beneath him, before he fell and landed with another sound that you could not hear but only see. Softer, slower, it was graceful in a way. His coat spread around him and his arms outflung. Face to the sky, as if he might have been looking back at you now, at last.

The driver must have known what had happened, he must have been aware of what he'd done, but he didn't slow and he didn't speed up either; he just kept going, down to the end of the next block, through a green light this time, and on, until you lost him, beyond the buildings that rose up to block your line of sight. There was the blue sky. And the warm sun on your arms. And your own face reflected back at you, in the window glass. You did what anyone would do. You reached for the phone.

Below, the scene had changed. Another woman was kneeling next to him first; then she was sitting in the street, cross-legged, close. She was leaning over him, she was caressing his hair, and she was talking to him, quietly consoling him. Later people would tell me about this, as if I might find some comfort in hearing how she didn't hesitate, she didn't question, she just emerged and went to him. She was a nurse, maybe, or a doctor even, or she was a minister, a woman of God in some way. Or a mother. She was someone who thought of him and waited with him, while the others all stood back and gawked, hand on mouth, or they turned away, sickened by the blood, the ruin of his face, and the tangle of his limbs, bent all wrong. One man took it upon himself to give chase, and he ran after the car for a couple of blocks, but it had already turned the corner and was gone.

2010 Ford Escort, white, sunroof. You called 911. Yours was the first report. At the trial nine months later, they played it back to us, and we heard your precise description of that car. There could be no mistake.

By the time the ambulance arrived, my husband was dead.

When we were first married, we had a small house consisting of two small bedrooms at the back, a bathroom, living room, breakfast nook, and kitchen. That was all. I loved the kitchen and the nook. Especially the glass doors on the cabinets with all our new china and crystal gleaming on the shelves behind them.

I got stoned on Saturday mornings and cleaned the house. My father-in-law dropped by after his store closed at noon. He sold surgical supplies. Catheters and bedpans. Calipers, wheelchairs, pillows, scales. Artificial breasts that you could cradle in the palm of your hand. Our conversations wandered. He came to think of me as vague, insubstantial, smoky, but he didn't know the half of it.

His wife, my mother-in-law, did not like me much. She favored my husband's former girlfriend, who was from someplace out west but had come to visit once and had charmed them all with her presence. She was beautiful, all right, and she had a body that everyone talked about after she'd left. That was the summer before I met him. When I was living out in California with a boyfriend of my own.

Many years later my mother-in-law fell down in her garden, and after that she couldn't talk, so I would go over to her house and wheel her around and talk and talk, and she would not be able to answer me back. Except to say, "I wonder." Or, "Oh my."

There was a coldness that came over me almost the day after our wedding. I didn't want him to touch me. His breath shivered at my throat or in my ear and made the hair on my arms stand up. I pushed him away before I could think what I was doing, and then I was sorry that I'd hurt his feelings, but there was nothing to do about it; that was just the way it was. After all those months we'd spent together the summer after the one with the girlfriend's visit, when we camped across the country and we were in our tent together every night, now we had a house and a new brass bed all our own. He stayed up late into the night, watching television and lighting matches, setting small fires in the ashtrays for me to find the next morning. Charred pages from the *TV Guide* went up in flames while I slept, deeply dreaming in our brass bed. Dreams so vivid and complex that I remembered them for years afterward, and they still come back to me again in the middle of the day sometimes, like a kind of déjà vu.

I was still in school then. He had a job he went to every day.

One night I told him, I said, "You know, if it weren't you, it would be somebody else."

Once when I was stoned and cleaning the house, before my father-in-law came by, I heard a voice behind or within or on top of the vacuum cleaner's noise, and I couldn't tell if it was in my head or if it was real, just that over the hum there was a sound like a radio announcer, that voice going on and on, flat vowels like a sportscaster, rising and falling, but I couldn't exactly make out the words. This went on all day, in the background of whatever else I was hearing, and then after that it came and went until one morning I was driving to class in a snowstorm and I couldn't see, so I had to pull over and wait for the snow to lighten up. I was under an overpass, and suddenly the voice was gone, and it was so quiet and cold that I wondered if I'd died or something and then after that I missed the voice in a way, but it never came back, and I stopped smoking pot then, which made my Saturday afternoon conversations with my father-in-law so much less interesting that after a while he quit coming by at all.

I wanted to paint our bathroom midnight blue, but I used oil paint on latex, or maybe it was the other way around. Anyway, it wouldn't stick and I painted it over and over again, but I didn't understand what was happening or what I was doing wrong. I didn't figure this out until many years later, when we were living in a much bigger house, with kids and dogs and cats and all that, and the painter who was working on our new addition told me about the difference between latex and oil, and I remembered, but at the time I know I thought it was in some way my fault.

The windowsill in our little bedroom in that first small house was rotted, and my husband started to pick at it, making it worse and worse until he had no choice but to take the window out altogether. He meant to replace it, but it was not a standard size, so he cut away the wall and made the window into a door instead, which then was a door that went nowhere, so he built a deck out there and invited his parents over for a barbecue when it was done. I used the good china, and his mother broke the last of our crystal glasses. She dropped it in the sink, but she didn't apologize. After they left we made love out on the deck, under the stars, early in April, too early really to be eating outside. It was cold and that's why his folks left early, not because of anything I said and not because of the broken glass. He and I sat out there anyway, and we smoked a joint and then I was on him, licking his throat. We were good from then on. Like we'd worked something out somehow.

If you hadn't called, someone else would have, and others did too, but you were the first to report the accident, and so you were the one they wanted to talk to, and you were the one who identified the car, so it was your description along with the license plate observed by someone else that led to the arrest of the kid who had been behind the wheel. He probably would have turned himself in anyway. Or so he said. He knew he'd made a mistake—a terrible mistake—a bunch of terrible mistakes—one on top of the other—and once he was clear of the scene, he could see that he was not going to be able to hide or run. He was only in high school, he was just a kid, where could he go? Except home to his parents to wait for the police to catch up, which they did. A couple of hours is all it took, and so by lunchtime he was in jail.

While I was at the morgue, you were answering questions up there in the hotel room, because the police wanted to hear what you had seen, and they wanted to see how it must have looked to you. Your description of the car and the accident itself. Just before and then the moment of, and afterward. And when they saw how upset you were—telling it over and over again, one moment to the next just as I have already described it myself, and as I have heard it from you too, when you had to tell it all again in court—when your strength weakened and you began to falter, you paled and started to break down, come apart, only then did they think to ask: Did you know him? And then you fell, as if from the great height of your remove, your overview, your omniscience, to the floor of the affair. And then you couldn't speak, but only nodded. Yes.

We moved to the bigger house, on the other side of town, in a better neighborhood. He had a good job and I was working too, and we had enough money then to do just about anything we wanted to do, pretty much. The bedroom in that house was called a master suite, and it had a chair by the window that looked out over the backyard, to the fence and the alley and the back sides of the houses beyond, where music drifted to us from an open window. This was in the summertime.

He was asleep in the bed on the other side of the room. His hands on his chest. Sleeping on his back like that, he would be snoring soon. The television was on, the volume low. The colors poured over his face.

I fixed myself another gin and tonic and sat in the chair, with my back to him. The music from somewhere else had stopped, and I missed it. The alleyway was still. The rain was soft at first, a drizzle that quickly picked up and thickened to a full downpour. A back door opened, spilling light onto the grass, and that created a shimmer in the wall of falling rain. A young man stepped out. He was shirtless, barefoot, in jeans. He dropped down from the porch to the grass and loped along the walkway to his car. He climbed in and rolled the windows up, then ducked through the rain, back to the shelter of the porch. He stopped there, just under the overhang where it was dry. His skin gleamed in the light. His hair was dark, cut short on top and in the front, left to grow out longer in the back as was the style then. He lit a cigarette and folded his arms across his chest and smoked and watched the rain, until he flicked the butt out into it, then turned and melted into the shadows of his house.

I knew who he was, in passing. I'd seen him go to his car in the mornings. He waved sometimes. Said hi now and then. He talked to my husband once, about a carburetor. Said he was twenty and still in school, studying anthropology or somesuch. This was when I was forty. I worked out the dates and counted back to when

I figured he was born, when I was twenty and still in school myself and dating the former boyfriend, who didn't want to think about the future, who had other plans, who didn't want to be tied down, and who gave me three hundred dollars to do what needed to be done.

You were the witness. You saw it all. For how many years had you been watching us from afar? How much did he tell you? About me. About us. Or did you talk of something else? On the nights when the two of you met, in one hotel or another, when he told me he would be elsewhere and with others, traveling on business, meeting clients, making a sale. Did he complain about me?

The kid behind the wheel was in his senior year of high school, with plans to go to college. A scholar. An athlete. His mother's favorite son. His father's promise. They asked for leniency because of all that. They tried to make me see. One life already ended, why ruin another? A mistake in judgment, the light first and then that he had kept on going after. But he was young. He was a kid, and who of us has not made a bad choice now and then, along the way? Did I have children? they wanted to know. Could I understand that part of it, at least?

In the newspapers and on the news, the whole story. The sympathies went to you, who loved him, who had to be the witness, who saw it all, from above, from afar, where there was nothing you could do but make the phone call, summon help, and then testify that yes, that was the car.

Someone looked at you and, having heard the story, was surprised to find that you aren't beautiful. You're not even young. And they wondered out loud, What did he see in her?

But time passes. Attention moves on. The story of the day is soon forgotten.

We bury him. We prosecute the boy. And then someone writes a check, payable to me.

The wind has been blowing in the canyon tonight, and it is fierce. Sometime around three a.m. the power goes out. I have the dog, so although I'm alone I feel safe, and when she stands at the door, I let her out. The city below this house, the canyon and the hills around, everything is dark.

I try to keep an eye on the dog, but she's black and I can't see her in the tangle of the back garden, the ferns and palms and jade. I have a flashlight, and I recently replaced the batteries, because there's been talk of earthquakes, what with the wind and the heat and the woman on the news telling us that chances are good that one will hit us soon. One month, a year, ten. Depends on what you mean by soon.

I step outside. There is no sound. I look up to see a plane passing overhead. I watch it for a second and then I run the flashlight over the yard, and there is the dog, also looking up and watching that plane on its way to somewhere else.

If this were a film, I think, just at this moment, just as we are here, the dog and I, and we are watching that plane, it would explode. This would be the beginning of the disaster, catastrophe, apocalypse, or whatever is the story, and a piece of the plane would fall and fall and hit me and knock me down dead. My husband, the main character in the film, the star of it, the hero, he would hear the terrible sound of that and the dog barking, going nuts, echoing across the darkened canyon, and he would quickly find me, in the garden, on the ground. That would be the beginning of the plot. I don't know what happens next.

This isn't how it goes, though. Not this time anyway. The plane just keeps on going toward its intended destination, safe and sound. I bring the dog inside. The power comes back and with it the lights. I fix myself a cup of coffee. The day dawns as usual. I get the newspaper and go back upstairs to bed, but he's still not here.

I wonder, I think. And, *Oh my.*

WHAT WE FORGET

~~~~~~

What we remember

For her it was the days that followed the first catastrophe. The first failure. The first hospitalization. The beginning of the end. The oxygen pump hissed and thumped, and she thought it was music playing. Some techno-pop thing turned low and going on in the background. Some dreary song, repetitive, dull, the kind of music she used to listen to when all was well and she was driving his car, buzzing on Diet Coke, and taking the long way around into town to get something or other, just for the sake of being out. The hiss and the thump on the radio—her heart kept pace with it. She was happy then and all things seemed sharp, bright, filled with promise and purpose. The diamond on her finger, gleaming in the sun. His smile. His teeth. The shine of his skin that paled, then turned dusky. His nose blue first, then purple. The bruise on the back of his leg that never had a chance to brighten back to yellow again. It was spring when he fell the first time. Winter the second. The year turned and by the end of the next summer, it was over. By fall the closets had been cleaned, the drawers emptied, the children were gone, the friends too. By fall she was alone. And then everybody wanted to know: Will you stay? Or sell the house? Find something smaller? She has a son in New York and a daughter in California, so there was no reason for her to stay put. You can travel now, they said. There is money. You're set. But the last thing she wanted, she said, was to be alone.

What we forget

For me it was the smell. Which after the first weeks of my first wife's illness I didn't notice anymore, except when I'd been out, which was hardly ever anymore. I knew what was in store, and I didn't want to leave her. I wanted to be there. I had to be there, I thought, so even a short trip to the store, an errand, a drive to the post office was enough to put me into a sweat. I could never shake the pressing urge to get back, and only then, coming in from outdoors, did I notice the smell, which I soon forgot again. When she died, finally, I was there, waiting, watching. The sun was high in the sky and bright in the window, and so I'd pulled back the curtains, to bathe her and myself in light. Later I threw open the window too, though this was in midwinter and the house was freezing when the hospice aide showed up, bustling in, a whirlwind of exclamation and hands, her coattails flying out behind her, to find my wife, cold, white, still on the bed and me asleep in the chair.

I forgot the smell and the silence. There was no question for me. I sold the house immediately. I took a room at the hotel.

She was at the bar. And that was how we met.

What we forget

For me it was the details. The daily this and that of living with a person. A stranger, really. A woman, mysterious and alien, in her way. The small things about her that I'm still learning every day. At first this is what drew me in and I never wanted to think of it as a trap, she some exotic flower opening feathered jaws, hidden barbs, to devour me; although there was a part of me then that longed to be devoured... subsumed... I don't have the word for it. Absorbed, maybe. I wanted to lose myself in her, at first. Forgetting the details, the way she might look at me, the questions she might ask. Her sudden fits of temper, how easily frustrated she can be, slamming a door or throwing a glass, angry at an inanimate object as if it has a personality and intentions— she takes its intractability personally. Her clothes in a pile on the closet floor. She'll get to them, she says, and shuts the door. Her shoes, scattered, and I trip over them. Her hair clogs the shower drain. And all of that makes me wonder why I couldn't leave well enough alone, spend some time living on my own, getting on by myself, maybe I would have liked that, or I'd have learned to like it anyway. But no. The grief and the strangeness of it assaulted me, it blinded me, I have come to understand since. Sugar on the countertop, spilled. Crumbs on the floor. She is not a tidy person. She doesn't notice things. The spatters on the bathroom mirror. Sometimes she snores, which appalls me. I lie next to her, listening to the hum of her breathing. Pig-like, it is. Honestly.

What we forget

For her it's things. Objects. Her glasses. Her keys. The grocery list. The letter to be mailed. Her watch. Her hat. Her gloves. There's always something and we're always going back for it. Setting out and then at the first stoplight, she begins. Sometimes later. She'll start, hiccup, Oh! And remember. So we'll have to turn around and go back. At first it was a joke. I thought for a while that maybe she was doing it on purpose. And then I tried to second-guess it. Going over a list. Which made her mad. Asking her, counting on my fingers. Do you have, did you remember: phone, wallet, license, credit card, the bottle of wine for our host?

We're on our way to a party that neither of us wants to attend, but she said yes anyway because her oldest friend will be there, and her sister too. The two of them, who always look at me askance as if to say, She could have done better, you know. And you're a very lucky man.

Usually by this time, ten minutes from the house, she'll be digging in her purse, lips tight, eyes wide. I can't look at her; I keep my own eyes on the road. It's raining and the wipers are going crazy, so loud that the radio is no use—and the car isn't the cozy refuge that I'd like it to be. Her bare shoulders and her perfume, her hair stiff with spray. Her hands folded in her lap. Pearls glowing at her throat. The swish of her stockings when she crosses her legs.

I splash around a corner, onto the avenue. Spatters of red from the other cars' taillights glisten in the rain. The traffic has stopped because of something up ahead, an accident or a traffic light gone out in the storm. I wish we'd just stayed home. A quiet evening together, just the two of us. A drink in the living room, like those times when we were first together. Her all dressed up and me too. So formal, we were then. I thought she was too shy, too reserved, and that this trait was going to show up elsewhere, in bed for example, where she would be modest about her aging body, ashamed of perceived flaws. But it was nothing like that. She surprised me. Slipping out of her dress and standing there, open, for me to see. This is who I am, what I've got, it's yours if you want it. Her expression frank. Ready for anything. Watching to see whether I winced or turned away in any way. But I didn't. Of course not. I took her up on the offer and then again and again—until there it was, I was caught, and we were married and now this. She has begun to stir. I can feel it coming. I creep the car forward. Rain pounds us and I can't see much more than the taillights of the cars up ahead. She's turned to look at me. Then away. I'll wait for her to speak, I think. Someone honks behind us. I shake my head and mutter, "As if."

She looks at me again, and I can't help it, I glance back and see the panic in her eyes.

I sigh. "What is it?"

She shakes her head. Tears glistening. Her hands clenching now in her lap.

I brake suddenly, jolting her forward. She puts a hand on the dash to brace herself, but that's not necessary. The traffic moves but I don't budge. That car behind me honks again. I glare at the rearview mirror, as if that might help. I mutter again, "Fuck off."

She's looking at me again. Her hair, softened by the damp, has fallen. Her teeth are bared, revealing the chipped tooth that I found so charming once. Another flash of panic in her face. She's pleading, "Please?"

Before we left tonight, I asked her—we went through all of it, as has become my habit now. "Do you have everything?" Her flash of annoyance, exasperation. "Yes, of course, I do," she said. As I went on, all the way through the whole list. Purse. Keys. What else is there? Every time this happens, I have something else to add to the list. Sweater. Hat. Checkbook. Camera. It's endless and it changes. "But why would I have a camera with me tonight?" she asked. Shaking her head and looking at me as if I was the one who was losing his mind. But then smiling because she's that way, naturally cheerful. "Silly," she said. Clucking. Nipping a kiss at my cheek. Bustling off to get her coat. Umbrella. The gift. Map. Bottle of wine. The champagne. The casserole. Whatever it was she meant to bring along.

This time there's been a change in all this. Because it's not what she's left behind but what she's left un-done. The back door open. The dog in the yard. It could have been anything, but tonight it's the dog.

That driver is leaning on his horn again as the gap ahead widens. I can see him in the rearview mirror. He's gesturing as someone else slips around in front of us, into the gap I've left. I jerk forward as if to make up for that, feeling the anger surge through me now too, then pull over to the right and keep on going. She has a hand over her mouth as we bolt along the shoulder, and the rain is making it that much harder for me, for every-body. She cries out my name; but I can't stop, furious, I want to tear the steering wheel apart, I'd be happy for an accident just now: some catastrophe for me to pour my rage into. My hand on the horn. Get the fuck out of my way, through my teeth. At night I grind them. Or clench them. One thing or the other. I used to do this when I was younger too. Cracked the molars, had to have them all replaced. They don't break anymore but my jaw throbs.

The shoulder narrows until I have no choice but to turn off, and immediately I can see it's a mistake. This road won't get us back, it's curving off, and we're going completely the wrong way, the lights of town are dim-ming behind us now. The rain, the dark, and she's got ahold of the door grip, her feet are braced against the floor. My anger steams in the small space of the car. I take a curve too fast, fishtail, and slow. When I look over at her, I can see her eyes are wide with fear. I roll to a stop. We both say it at the same time: I'm sorry. Hers a whimper, mine stronger. I say, We'll go home. She nods. The rain is still coming down hard. The head-lights crack the darkness ahead of us. I could turn around but not here, the road is too narrow. Nothing but empty fields on either side. She gazes out the window, picturing the dog out in the rain, I guess. He's okay, I tell her. She nods. We're creeping forward again now. My anger has dissipated, and with it my courage has gone too. This is my fault. If I had stayed put, if I'd kept my head, we'd be through that knot of traffic by now. I could have talked her out of it, maybe, her worry for the dog. We might have got somewhere with all that. Or I could have found another way to get back. Or... but never mind, because here we are. The road drops down, then rises. There will have to be a turnoff soon. This road has to go somewhere, doesn't it?

Out here in the farmland, there are all these little towns, one after another, houses huddled around town squares. We're bound to come upon one sooner or later, and sure enough before you know it, I see the lights ahead. I turn to her and smile. Again I say, I'm sorry. We'll find a place. Pull over. Stop and go in. This will be something new for us. An adventure. A drink. Dinner. It will be romantic. I'll hold her hand. I'll kiss her. Maybe there will be a shop, and I can buy her something. I reach out, brush her cheek with my thumb. She likes that. I love you, I say, and she nods, like she already knows that. Or she agrees. Or she loves me too.

This little place turns out to be not much more than an intersection with a stop sign and a gas station on one corner. There is no town square. No restaurant. No bar. But at least the lights are on in the station and a silhouette of someone sitting behind the cash register in the window. The rain is letting up too, as I turn and pull up to the pump and stop. I have plenty of gas. We don't need gas. I don't forget things like that.

She's out of the car before I can say anything. One hand covers her head as she skips across the pavement and up the steps and inside, where I can see her form outlined in the window, beyond a display of motor oil cans stacked up to form a pyramid that mimics the pyramid that is the logo of the brand. I don't know why I remember this detail, or why I mention it, when I'm telling the story again, of how we stopped here and she went inside, to use the bathroom. No, there was no argument. And, no, I was not angry. By then I wasn't upset anymore and neither was she.

When I look again, she's coming outside, holding a key attached to some kind of paddle, or a ruler maybe, or some piece of wood. To discourage theft I guess, but who would want to keep that key? She's using it to unlock the restroom door. Just then the wind picks up and blows her hair around. She turns on the light and goes in and closes the door behind her.

I'm thinking, if only she had turned, if only she'd looked back at me, then maybe I could wait for her. But she didn't do that. She trusts me.

I haven't even turned off the motor. We don't have cellphones. She's forgotten her purse, left it here in the car with me. I don't back up. The attendant does not come out. The rain stops. I wait a few moments. Awhile. I can't say how long I wait. That's what I remember, but the attendant will say I didn't wait at all. That I drove off right then, and I left her there. I can't say why.

The house is dark except the light at the back, in the kitchen by the door, the one she always leaves on. The dog is not in the yard, and the gate is open, and I'm thinking she was right to worry about him, but then I hear the barking and as I let myself in, I am able to settle back into my old certainty about the way things are. The dog bounds past me, squats to pee on the grass, then comes back again, and he's sitting at the door, waiting for me to let him in. He's wet now, tracking muddy paw prints on the white kitchen tiles. The gleaming surfaces. Everything in its place. One cupboard door has been left open, and I tap it with a finger so it smacks shut, and the sound of this seems to echo in the empty house. I glance at the phone, but she won't be calling, not yet. I imagine her confusion. The clerk looking up as I drove away, thinking at first that she was with me, worried at first about the key on the paddle, then going to check and instead finding her. Bewildered. She will wait. She'll be thinking there's some explanation for why I've left her there, but she can't remember what it is.

The clerk says she did not come in, but just handed him the key and told him she was fine. She lived not far, she said. She would walk. Now that the rain had stopped and it was a lovely night. The sky cleared pretty quickly. The stars were bright and the moon was high and bright too, so if she'd wanted to she could have easily found her way.

I have explained it as best I can. I was fed up but I was going to go back. I just wanted to teach her a little lesson. Self-reliance, maybe. I was only going to pull around to the side, into the shadows where she couldn't see me. Confuse her that way. Scare her a little, maybe. But then I just kept going. There was music on the radio and that was nice. I thought I would turn around pretty soon, but then I didn't do it.

You can't say I meant her any harm, exactly.

It's not a crime, is it, to leave your wife alone somewhere at night?

DEAR MR. FANTASY

Memory is a funny thing, not because of what comes to mind, but because of what doesn't. All the moments, all the faces, all the places we've forgotten. They're in there somewhere, aren't they? Is it only a matter of access? The right word said, the exact scent, the taste, the touch, the sound.

Take Isabel Cooke. Here she is, in her house in her town in her world as it is now, with her husband dead a year. All the friends and colleagues who came around at first, to honor him and comfort her, have slipped back into their own lives again, leaving Isabel to fend for herself, supposing she must be over her grief by now.

And maybe so. She might have moved on, as she's heard someone put it, though moving on for her is going to take some packing first, because she was married to Alan for thirty-two years, and they were sweethearts for eight years before that, so forty years altogether, and only the one without him now to balance all that against. Even in dog years, it isn't enough.

She has plenty to keep her busy. Her house. Her garden. Her car, her bank account, her clothes, her dishes, her linens, her books, her papers, her furniture, and yet it's all of it tangled up with him. There are associations everywhere, even with the photographs removed. The lamp he made. The table he repaired. The cabinets he painted. He's here in everything.

Watching her, it seems.

She sits at the table nursing a cup of tea, warming her hands, and listening to the quiet that defines her loneliness—no sound of his footsteps, no creak on the stairs, no water running in the shower. A silence so complete, it hums. Or she stands at the window, arms folded over herself, and peers out at the road. As if he might be coming home. The car in the lane. The hand on the gate, the step on the porch, and how he'd greet her. A kiss on the forehead. The same old hello and how was your day and what's for dinner, and you expect me to eat this slop?, and wipe that look off your face. What look? Nothing she did, nothing she said, but something had made him mad.

But that's all over now, and she can feel it fading more every day. She watches television and movies. She looks at magazines, photographs, and paintings. She stares at the smallest thing—a leaf, a tree, a butterfly, a bird—to burn new pictures into her mind until they become so clear that everything else gets dim.

And then the dog. And then the phone call.

First, the dog. His dog, hers now. Heavy body, bandy legs, like Alan himself. The broad brow. The powerful shoulders. Small hips, balls hanging. He's a pit bull, full grown and beset with bad habits that Alan never bothered to train out of him, because already he was dying and there wasn't time. The dog turned out to be a companion, a comfort to him in those last days, after the fall, when he was bedbound downstairs in the front room that had been converted to contain him. The TV set just so and on all day, screaming at him because he was deaf a little and asleep a lot. The leg would heal and the ribs, too, but not the head. She came downstairs that morning—like Christmas—to find him with the dog there beside him, snarling when she tried to get close, whispering his name. Then alarmed and louder, but Alan's jaw was hanging and his eyes were open, and he was cold and clearly dead.

It took food to get the dog to come away. A steak, as in a cartoon. She thawed it in the microwave and then stood there at the door with the summer a raucous green beyond, teeming with life, as if in taunt to him. Holding the door open with her foot and calling to the dog, who scrabbled up and bounded, sliding, down the hall, all memory of master gone, replaced by the smell of meat. Tossed out into the backyard, and then the door slammed after him.

From there, a cascade of event. Too fast, too jumbled to sort clearly. Phone calls and visitors. Arrangements, papers signed, flowers, casseroles, a black dress, and a black umbrella. The bed removed and the house put back the way it was, the way she liked it, as she cleared her husband out of here one room at a time. So now, twelve months later, in high summer once again, there's hardly any trace of him left at all.

Except the dog, who remains a constant reminder, as if Alan planned it that way. Looking at her, with Alan's eyes. Chin on his paws. And not a pretty dog. Not even a friendly dog. Not a companion to her. A watch dog maybe. Every bag of kibble she buys and lugs from the store to the car, then drags from the car into the house, is a resentment.

The dog dozes by the back door, spread out, belly to the cool floor. It's midmorning and the summer heat is starting to build. The garden is a riot of vegetables that she will never be able to eat. Maybe it will rain. Isabel Cooke is in her kitchen drinking tea and making a list. Soon she'll go out on the porch to read while the bees buzz the flowers and the sun creeps across the sky.

And that would be that, a day like any other day, except the phone rings and she jumps and the cup clatters out of its saucer. The dog startles awake and is on his feet, barking deliriously. He slams into the door and through the screen, leaves it hanging.

When the machine picks up, what she hears is Alan's voice, like a ghost slamming into her. "We're not here. Leave a message. Maybe we'll call you back." And then a silence, in which she sits, frozen, while the tea runs off the edge of the table and drips onto the floor, and the dog's barking fades into the distance.

Then: "Isabel? I don't... Well, this is Duffy. Duffy Branch. I know it's been awhile, and I'm sorry I didn't call sooner, but I only just now heard. And so I'm calling to say... Well... I'm sorry, I guess. But... You can call me back if you want."

And then, his number. The click of the machine. The tape whirring, resetting itself. A beep. A new message. Beep. A new message. The light flashes.

Beep. Beep.

Duffy Branch.

Once he's out the door, the dog is gone. Charging after the kids who have been huddled behind the bushes at the side of the backyard. These kids who are drawn here to the widow's house at the end of the lane, where the woods thicken above the creek that they've been fishing all morning until now, on a dare, they've crept up into her yard, to peek through the bushes for a glimpse of her. She's crazy, they've said, or heard their parents say. She killed her husband, didn't she? She's a witch. She will poison you or try to take you. She kidnaps kids and keeps them in her basement. She used to be a teacher, the meanest teacher you ever had, the one who would slap you and send you out into the hall. The one with the long nose and small mouth and sharp finger always pointing at you, or someone like you. And then they fired her. There was a scandal of some kind. The memory's not clear. It might not even have been her, it could have been someone else, but it doesn't matter, because these kids hear the stories and they tell them over and over, upping the ante, compounding the risks, until the little ones are properly terrified. Because then the dare can mean something. Go up there and ring the doorbell. Put this on the porch. Break a window. Steal something, anything. It's a test and if you're brave enough, if you can pass it, then we'll let you… What? Join the club. Be our friend. Be one of us.

Not figuring the dog. Or not mentioning him, because that's half the game, it's half the fun—send a kid into her yard or up to the door, then watch what happens, as the dog comes bounding out, a thick ball of muscle and rage, through the screen and onto the porch and into the yard. You hardly have time to turn, to change your mind, to run back to the woods with that hell dog at your heels, his breath huffing, his paws pounding, and your friends, if that's what they are, all watching and laughing as you fly across the grass, yelping in terror. He leaps and you fall, hard, the wind knocked out of you.

He's on top of you, gnashing, though he won't bite. He sits on your chest, his face to your face. Slobbering. Panting. Grinning, it seems. You've passed the test. You're all right.

She listens to the message four times before she writes the number down. And then once more to be sure she has it right. Not that she's going to call him back. No, that isn't her intention, not yet. Finally she erases the message and thinks again about changing her own message—removing Alan's voice from the machine. She's aware of the dog, barking in the woods, and the cries of children too. She unplugs the machine from the wall and then from the phone. Wraps the cord around it and puts it in the trash. Gathers the bag, which is not quite full, cinches it tightly shut, carries it to the backdoor, sets it on the porch. Puts a new bag in. Looks out the window to see a flash of color beyond the bushes. The children, she assumes, playing.

By the time she's fixed the screen, she knows she'll call Duffy back. It's only a matter of time. Not whether, but when.

Not long, as it turns out. She puts the tools away and looks out at the woods to see whether the kids are gone, to see if the dog is coming back. His representative, his spy, as if Alan were still there, watching her. She doesn't like the scrutiny.

By now she has the number memorized. The paper is folded in her pocket, but she takes it out to look at it again, to be sure she has it right. Three rings, four, five, and now she's panicking at the choice that's been presented: Will she hang up or will she leave a message of her own? But the phone just rings and rings, as if he doesn't even have a machine or a service, and for a bit this seems all right, listening to the ringing. It's soothing, in a way, and she gets used to it. She doesn't do anything, just hears it, dreamily, as if she just might sit there like that forever.

Until he picks up. "What?"

So startled, she doesn't know what to say, at first. Then, "Duffy?"

She remembers his teeth, the gap between them that was supposed to mean something. And his eyes. She's wondering whether he still has his hair. "It's Isabel."

He says he didn't know about Alan, or he would have called sooner. He only heard yesterday or last week or sometime. And, what happened? And, are you all right?

This takes her aback. That he would show up like this, out of the blue, after so many years, to ask her that, now.

"I'm fine." Which isn't exactly true, but he seems glad to hear it anyway. His voice warms, and now she's telling him how it happened, this story that she's told so many times, but he brushes it aside. He doesn't want to talk about Alan, he wants to talk about her. He's remembering, he says, their morning ride. So many years ago. It was that summer and he calls out the year.

There was a party, an all-night party, and... He tells her what he remembers, a story she listens to. But. No. That wasn't her, was it? She doesn't want to disappoint him, but... When, again? "I don't think..."

She wants to remember. She wants it to be true.

But now there's someone banging at the front door. She looks up in fear. Caught, as if she's been doing something she shouldn't, and she tells him, "I have to go. I'm sorry." And then hangs up on him.

At the door: the dog, on a leash. The kid, bloodied. The father, threatening.

"Your fucking dog. My son. I'll sue."

He unhooks the leash, and the dog bounds in, back to the kitchen, collapses on the floor near the stove, panting. Seeming to grin. Looking at her, as if, she thinks, he knows.

It might have ended there. Both the phone call and the angry parent at the door. Blips on the screen. Waves cresting, then gone. The long quiet time between events, the silence between the tick and the tock, erasing all reaction first and then even memory. She might forget he ever called, and the father, satisfied by his own righteousness and his own anger successfully vented—that could have been the end of it. Let well enough alone. The fracas faded; the dog slept. She sat at the kitchen table, eating her supper. Reading. Working a crossword. No one came to the door. The phone did not ring. This went on for days.

But now there is a package in the mail. She's not accustomed to anything other than flyers and bills—some of them addressed to Alan still, his name not yet erased from all the lists, and how would they know if she didn't take the trouble to write and tell them? It's a padded envelope with her name printed large, front and center, and Duffy's smaller on the upper left. She carries it into the living room and sets it on the chair. The dog, following, wants her to hand it over to him, like Alan reading her mail before she could get to it herself.

There is no note. Nothing but a CD—Traffic, "Mr. Fantasy"—and a photograph, clipped from a magazine. She puzzles over these only for a moment before she realizes: This is the song they listened to, on that sunrise drive, and this was his car—a 1967 TR4A. The top was down. It was August, so there might have been a first chill of fall that early in the morning. The music loud. Her hair long and blowing. His hands on the wheel, and the way the car hugged the curves. From the farmhouse where the party was, around the long bend, and then over the bridge. A left turn into the park. The woods thick. Wet, with morning. They'd been up all night and they were high, but it was wearing off, a headache coming on.

On Saturday there's a postcard in the mail, and Isabel wonders if the mailman noticed and read it and now is speculating about her. Whether he'll tell someone and it will get around and then they'll have one more thing to laugh at about her, the old widow with a man in her life again.

The photo on the front—a park. The scene is summer. The black road winds into a cascade of full-leaved trees. They would have left the party at the house at the end of a back lane through the fields that run alongside the river and takes you to the highway, where the entrance to the park is. Heading west then, with the sunrise behind them. The sky purple up ahead and lilac at your back, yellowing at the rim where the sun begins to glimmer. The top down. He in a T-shirt and a cap. Bell bottom jeans and bare feet. His hair long, curly at the ends. She in a summer dress and sandals.

On the back of the card he has written, "Remember this?"

She stares at it for a long time. She puts it down and picks it up and puts it down again. She can see herself getting into the car. He opens the door for her, smiling. It's an ironic gesture, old-fashioned.

But she has nothing before that. How they happen to be together. How he invites her to go with him. The others strewn about the house and porch and yard in various states of bacchanalian repose. Some passed out. One in the hammock. Maybe that's Alan.

But Isabel is wide awake and so is Duffy, and he shares his cigarette. Then as the sky begins to change he says, "Do you want to take a ride?" And she says, "Sure." That simple. So he pulls her to her feet, and she follows him across the grass.

She can get herself into the car with him. She can get the top down and the headlights on. He backs around, his arm across the seat, his hand on the wheel, spinning. A stick shift? And then they're heading up the long drive; they're turning into the lane. The headlights first, now the music. The wind in her hair. His eyes on the road. She can get them right up to the entry to the park that way. His blinker flashing.

But that's as far as she can go. Sitting on a rock beside the creek, holding the post card. Studying the picture. Turning it over to read his question again. "Remember this?" While the dog rolls in manure.

By the time she gets back to the house she's decided it's time to get rid of the dog. While she hoses him off she considers how she might do it. When she turns off the water, he shakes himself dry and jumps around. Playful, happy, so she can't be mad at him. In this, too, he reminds her of Alan.

In the phone book there are two listings for animal shelters. One here in town and another just off the interstate, twenty miles away. Tomorrow she'll get him in the car and drive him over there. Say as little as possible. Just leave him and come home, she thinks, and then that will be the end of that.

He follows her upstairs to bed. He's on the floor, sleeping, while she lies awake and watches the moon and hears an owl and sees the shadows of the trees moving in the wind.

In the mail the next morning, this time it's not a card, it's a letter.

Dear Isabel,

Have you got a memory yet? Any sparks? I propose a re-enactment. Just me and you. We'll retrace the now infamous route, cool? It did happen, as I've this burnt-in memory of returning to the farmhouse, and the rising sun to the east, aglow on your blond hair, blowing in the wind.

The dog goes willingly into the car. She leaves the back window open, and as they drive he has his head out, tongue hanging, eyes squinting in a way that makes him look like Alan laughing, which was rare.

She has the address and the town is small. The shelter is on a country road, down at the end of a long dirt driveway. The dog, getting a whiff of what's in store maybe, whines, then barks, then leans forward so his head is next to hers.

"Almost there," she says, to calm herself as much as him.

It's hot already and it will get hotter as the day wears on, but there is a lingering coolness in the shadows of the trees that hover around the low concrete building with the kennels at the back. She has the dog on a length of clothesline because she thought to leave his collar and tags at home. It should look like this is not her dog. She has her story ready—he's a stray, he just showed up. She put a flyer out, but no one called. Some talk about people and irresponsibility and abandoning their pets in these hard times, when you have to cut back somewhere if you want to keep your family fed.

It's not until she tries the door that she realizes there's no one here. She hums a bit in her frustration. The sign is clear as day—Monday: Closed. The dog is pulling at her, so she yanks him back and takes the rope off. She rolls it up as he bolts around the corner, stops to sniff, lifts his leg, then ambles on, hackles raised, toward a run where another pit bull is frantically throwing itself at the fence, teeth gnashing.

She doesn't stay to see what happens next, but turns, quickly, and hurries back across the grass and then the gravel, to the car. Her heart slamming, ears ringing. She slows at the top of the drive. A truck barrels past and she slams on the brakes. Dust roils behind her.

She waits. She watches in the mirror, expecting to see the dog come into the yard again, looking for her, for her car. Or the door of the building opening and someone stepping out, someone who has seen everything and knows what she's done, what she's trying to do. But there is nothing. No dog, no dog catcher. She puts on her blinker, looks both ways, then pulls out onto the highway again and heads back home, alone.

Now that dog is gone and she's by herself in the house, it's as it was when Alan died, those first days after, when it was still possible for her to imagine that he was just gone out somewhere and would be coming back again any minute. She tries to pinpoint when it was that that changed—the precise moment when she realized that no, not so, he's dead, Isabel, it's over—and recalls a morning when she woke and the sun was already streaming in the window and she could feel it, she just knew that now the world was all her own. She recalls the way she moved that morning, going about her business in the stillness of the house as if it had a personality itself and they were in cahoots, she and the house, in this their new emptiness, their new silence, in which anything could be said or thought or done, and it would always be her own.

It's like that again now, with the dog gone. She can think that nothing's changed. He's off somewhere outside, getting into trouble that will bring someone to the door to scold her for something that he's done, but she's responsible for. Or the phone will ring and someone will be complaining and telling her that whatever has happened, it's her fault and she must make amends. He chased a child or he tore through a garden or he pulled down some clothes from the line in somebody's backyard. Muddy footprints on the porch. A dead chicken in the yard. A pile of his stink steaming on the sidewalk. But no, now there won't be anymore of that.

So she should be happy. She should be feeling free. Except it isn't morning, it's night. And she's in bed and the empty house is really empty now, it's really all just hers. No Alan. No dog. For the first time, she's afraid. Her mind seethes, her body tenses and curls in on itself, and then, before she knows it, Isabel is weeping.

When the front door bangs, at first she doesn't

hear it, but when it bangs again and then the third time she stops her gurgling and lifts her face from the pillow where she's buried it to muffle the sobs, and holds her breath and listens. She creeps to the window to look out and expects to see a car in the driveway, pulling away now, or waiting. Again a sound. Someone is out there on the front porch. So now she's floating down the stairs—her face a mess, her hair wild—and as she's turning on the light it occurs to her: it must be the dog. He's found his way back. He's here and he wants in.

But no. No one is there. Or if they are, they're hiding. Did she lock the back door? Are all the windows closed? Could someone have come into the house somehow and now is hiding? Standing behind her, watching her, in the closet, in the basement, in the attic, behind the door.

She spends the rest of the night downstairs. In Alan's chair. With his shotgun across her knees.

When she wakes, it's with a sense of surprise that she's even slept at all. She's glad she's alone and no one, especially not Alan, has seen her this way, tangled in this panic and this doubt. He would have rolled his eyes and said, "'Twas ever thus, my dear." Taking the gun gently from her hands and putting it back in the front hall closet where it belongs, behind the winter coats and the umbrellas and the boots. "You're all right, Isabel," he'd say. "You're perfectly safe here. You'll be fine." It's a moment before she hears this and understands that she's been talking to herself, and maybe that scares her more than the idea even of someone there in the house watching her and waiting for the right moment to step out into the light and reveal himself as one who has come to inflict some kind of final harm.

But there is no one there. Isabel is alone, and that's all she wanted, isn't it? She turns on the lights, turns on the television, slaps around barefoot, busy with the business of making coffee and taking her vitamins and brushing her teeth and combing her hair. The TV is reporting traffic conditions in a larger town than this and weather in another state altogether. Farm reports and stock reports. News and commentary. While Isabel Cooke sits at the kitchen table with her hands cradling her mug, and behind the windows the sky brightens and the shadows recede, to reveal, in the front yard, beyond the dewy grass, the ruin of her garden. The plants trampled. Tomatoes smashed. The fence broken. The gate hanging on its hinges. There are muddy footprints in the grass. She stands on the back stoop staring at them, trying to figure, how many? One or two? Or twenty? These kids emerging from the trees, creeping across the lawn and then tearing into the garden in a mad wild frenzy of annihilation aimed at her. And in the middle of it a threadbare witch with a monster mask, hanging from a tree, arm raised, and finger pointing at the house.

We drove the back way around the lake. No one else was up. We left them sleeping, crashed around the house on sofas, in chairs, in beds, and on the floor, together or alone, and we two the only ones still awake. I took your hand. You followed me out to the car. We left the headlights off and rolled away, down the driveway to the road and down the road into the park. Your blond hair blowing. Your hand on my knee. The radio was playing, "Dear Mr. Fantasy," and I kissed you as the sun came up and the sky brightened into day.

PHIPP

~~~~~~

When Jackson Bale crossed the line to collide head-on with a ten ton semi-trailer truck on a Tuesday evening early in November, I was the one who stood up first at the emergency meeting and volunteered to go out to the farmhouse to feed the dog and bring it to the school for Jack's widow to take with her, back to the hometown in Iowa where his mother was waiting, where the funeral services were to be held, and where he would be buried in a plot near the ground that already held the remnants of his grandparents and his dad. Although there might have been some murmurs of doubt that floated around the room, no one had the nerve to flat out look me in the eye and tell me no, I was not the one to go. So I drove Charlie's old blue Volvo station wagon out there first thing in the morning, and I took my time with it, creeping along slowly— as if I believed that my own extreme caution could make a difference and bring a change to what was already over with and done.

I went by way of the Ridge Road, following along the same path that Jack himself had taken the night before, and I knew at just which of the curves the accident had occurred, because although his mangled Jeep was towed off almost immediately after his body had been extracted from it, the semi had to be left where it was until a special wrecker could be called. The windows of the cab were scarred with frost, and it was severed from its trailer, which lay overturned nearby. I noticed that an arrangement of orange and blue carnations had already been fastened to a standing portion of the toppled fence, adding an uneasy splash of color to the grimmer background of the fallow field that rolls off downhill toward the creek, and I knew that just as soon as the whole story of what had happened got out, there would be plenty of other lookie-loos showing up to ogle the sight firsthand and imagine the flash and burn.

As for me, I sucked in my breath and kept my eyes on the road, until the familiar sight of his name stenciled in black letters on the metal mailbox at the end of the driveway popped up to knock the air back into me and burn my cheeks just like a full hand smack to the face. Although there weren't any other cars around, still I went to the trouble to put on the blinker, signaling my intention well before I turned the Volvo in toward his house. Julia had left the front porch light on, but its otherwise welcoming glow was washed out and made feeble now by the dazzle of early morning sun already reflecting off the thin unbroken surface of that season's first sticking snow.

I took my time crossing the span of space between Charlie's car and Jack's front door, moving at the same slow and careful pace that I'd already been keeping, hands in my coat pockets and head bowed. The last thing anybody needed now was for me to lose my footing, slip and fall and crack my head. So focused was my attention on the cautious placement of my feet that I was all the way up to the door before I saw the black coonhound shivering on the stone stoop. He had been there for a while, waiting for someone like me to come along and let him in, unaware of how his world had been forever changed while he was out nosing around in the woods all night, the way hounds do. Or maybe he did understand everything after all, because he took one look at me, raised his head, and howled.

I was busy fumbling for the key that Mrs. Ayer had given me to get in. My hands were cold and stiff and would not cooperate with my will—I should have worn gloves. The dog had pulled himself up to his feet, but the wag of his tail seemed pensive. The key wouldn't turn, and he whined at me as I fiddled with it, so I stopped struggling for a moment and blew on my fingers to warm them. I took a deep breath to calm myself down, then turned back to the door again to work the key more slowly now, until at last the lock gave way, and the bolt slid out and then I was able, finally, to let myself in.

The hound glided past me toward the kitchen where he knew his dish was, but I lingered in the doorway for a second, looking into the main room of the house, taking in the evidence of the life that had so recently been carried on there as if it might go on like that forever. Jack's chair on one side of the fireplace and Julia's on the other. Magazines piled on the coffee table, a book lying open on the floor, the cracked red leather of the couch, and the bright green and yellow of an afghan thrown across its back. A still life composition of chess board, stereo speakers, television set, coffee mug, whiskey glass, potted plant. The this and that of the here and now that got me to thinking some more about the impermanence of all things in general.

I was not a stranger to the place. I knew my way around that house, inside and out, upstairs and down, but I had never had the occasion to be there on my own—not without Charlie first and not without Jack later—and anyway at that moment I would rather not have had a reason to remember how, on the eve of Charlie's deployment, Jack had stopped me in that doorway right there and, laughing, kissed me on the mouth for all to see. He was only trying to make the point that Charlie had a choice, but there it was—the silky brush of Jack's lips across mine, the grit of his whiskered chin against mine, the smell of scotch and tobacco on his breath mingling with the same on mine—and I kept going back to the pang of that first touch, even after they brought Charlie back home to us ten months later, all the way up until Jack's sudden and surprising engagement to Julia Radler last year, which was designed to put an end to it, once and for all.

But there I was again, stepping into that house and taking note of how the place had changed since those earlier days when none of us knew anything about what was going to happen to us next. This was not the home of a man all on his own anymore—special touches here and there told that. Desperado had come to his senses, and now there was a bowl of red apples on the table, a bunch of wildflowers in a milky blue vase, whimsical little crystal figurines gleaming on a glass shelf near the window.

The brass clock on the mantel chimed eight times, which meant that the morning chapel service would be starting up over at Stanley Hall, and I was glad to be here and not there as the girls filed in and jostled each other for a seat in the pews, their combined smell of wet wool and citrus shampoo, coconut lip gloss and patchouli perfume filling the air while Velma Briggs hammered out something desperately cheerful up front on the baby grand.

It would be up to Dean Bradley then to break the news to the girls, although some of them would no doubt have heard some bits and pieces of the story already. Amanda Wirth, whose father was a state trooper, for example. And what word they had would have spread quickly from one girl to the next, warped into a mystery as it traveled among them in a hiss of whispers. Some would have had the presence of mind to compare the stories they were telling, testing the details to determine what was true and what was not, but even they would have had to take it as a bad sign that Mr. Bale's car was not to be found in its assigned space in the parking lot this morning. That he hadn't been seen in his office or in the hallways as usual earlier. That he wasn't sitting in what was his customary place up on the dais now, and that the piano prelude was too loud and had been going on for too long, until finally Dean Bradley bustles in from the wings and moves to the lectern, where she taps the microphone with a finger, takes a breath, and solemnly eyes the assembled girls, who have all stopped talking and stopped breathing and gone still.

She wouldn't mince her words, that is not her style. Mr. Bale has been involved in an accident, she would be telling them, and at first they'd be thinking that was it, and he was all right after all, he was hurt, maybe, he was in the hospital even, and that was bad, but it was not the worst that could be. They would be waiting for her to tell them that the rumors were only that, but then when she goes on and confirms the truth, her voice hitching as she says the words out loud—Dean Bradley, who Charlie had named Her Majesty the Imperious Snow Queen because of the halo of white hair and the broad square shoulders, the unwavering gaze and the hard cold set of her jaw—when she seems to sob the words that tell them Jack is dead, then this will be what finally sets the girls off, and after that, pandemonium.

Some of them will react with anger, first. There will be cries of disbelief and bursts of tears, screams, explosive sobs. Dr. Larsen will have to be brought in, and Father Stephens will be there too. Classes will be cancelled—no geometry or biology or English lit today. Instead, the talk is going to have to be of Heaven and Hell, the Here and the Hereafter, and God's Will or Man's Fate, the ineluctable force that physics has on flesh. The flag at the edge of the Oval will be lowered to half-mast again. Some of the girls will beg to be allowed to go home, and arrangements are going to have to be made to accommodate them in that.

Even my most tentative movement into that room seemed to create too much of a ruckus in the stillness—as I reached across his chair to turn off a reading lamp, the air was disturbed by my presence, and dust motes swirled near the window where the sun had begun to break in through the curtains. So I moved slowly and I kept my head low, as I crossed the room and made my way up the stairs.

The master bedroom is in the far back corner of Jack's house; its high windows overlook the grassy yard with its dilapidated barn to one side and the acres of woodland that spread out on beyond. The closet door was open, revealing Julia's bright clothes on one side and Jack's familiar shirts and pants and jackets on the other, with his heavy shoes paired side by side on the floor below them. A pink silk robe that I hadn't seen before hung from a hook on the back of the door.

The sight of the unmade bed against the far wall felt like a violation of another kind, but I spent some time putting it to right, carefully folding the edge of the sheet back over the top of the taut blanket and placing the pillows just so, as in a hospital or a hotel, as if it were just some random place for any stranger to come along and lay his head down for a while. When I was finished with this chore, I turned back to the closet to have one last look at Jack's things, as a way of saying good-bye to all that, I guess. I poked at the shoulder of a wool tweed sport coat and watched the sleeve swing as if there were some life in it, and then I stooped and slipped my hands down into the cool void of his tooled leather boots. I held them like that as if I were holding him, but it wasn't so. I lifted them up then set them down again beside a pair of Julia's red satin flats. I stepped back to consider the effect of this—it looked like something of an apology, to my eye. I closed the closet door on the whole thing then, once and for all, and if I was feeling anything like a sting of tears just then, I quickly blinked them away. I had no right or reason in the world to be grieving for this man that I was not supposed to know.

Over at Stanley Hall, a policeman was posted just outside the iron gates, and a local news van was lurking at the curb across the street. I gave the officer my name and told him what I was there for, showed him my driver's license and all that other rigmarole, then waited for him to call somebody on his radio and get some kind of an okay before he would consent to open the gate and wave me in. From there I followed the long driveway that wound down through the woods and then opened up onto the grassy Oval at the end. The lot was full, so I had to park the Volvo next to the trash bins behind the Dining Hall.

I was aware of what I looked like to the two girls who were sharing a smoke in the woods and watching me as I started climbing up toward the Main Building at the far side of the Oval. Thin and tall and pale, I am not much to look at, but I do take up space. My hair is yellow and straight, neatly trimmed and only just beginning to recede. My eyes are soft—hazel gray or green or brown or blue, depending upon what else is going on around me. I know that to some of the girls in my classes I am a tragic figure—maybe even, from a distance, Byronesque. To others, I'm just another creep in a long black coat. I have the kind of face that people often say they think they've seen before. I am always reminding somebody of someone else that they know better than they know me. To the parents I am Mr. Phillips, but the girls all call me Phipp.

As I headed toward Main Hall, I thought of Jack crossing the campus just as I was doing then, striding the footpath with his hound at my heels. I was trying to summon up the sound of him calling to it, or of anybody else ever saying its name, but I couldn't hear the word in my mind. I stopped and checked his tag: "Pal." His name was Pal, and when I said it he looked at me like he was waiting for me to tell him something more, but I had nothing.

Dean Bradley was not in her office, but Mrs. Ayer was at her desk as usual. She was busy typing something, and very serious about it, hunched over her keyboard and pecking at it, stopping to give the screen an abrupt quizzical squint, then right back at it again. The most important work in the world, it must have been. I had to cough into my fist before she became aware of me standing there. Her face was round and flat, her eyes agog behind her glasses and her mouth a rosy wrinkled pucker, drawn tight as a cat's asshole. I gave her the house key and had planned to offer to hang on to the dog until Julia returned, but just then the phone rang, and Mrs. Ayer put up a finger to hush me as she reached to answer it. When I let go of his leash, the hound crossed the hall to nose and paw at Jack's office door, and I thought it best that I back off then and let someone else look after him now.

The girls were still there when I got back to the car. They saw that I was watching them watching me, but there was no reason for them to care. They waved to me, said something to each other, and then headed off arm in arm deeper into the woods, toward the bluff, which has a spectacular view of the river but is strictly off limits even for the seniors, without a chaperone. I might have called them back, but I knew they were unlikely to heed whatever I could have found it in myself to tell them. They had nothing to fear from me. They would know that all bets are off, and there are not going to be any demerits or detentions handed out for whatever anyone might decide to do now. There isn't much safety to be had anywhere anymore, not that I can see, and they are young enough still to think that the view alone is worth whatever risk it will take to get there to see it for themselves.

JUST SO

~~~~~~

I left Iris sleeping and went outside with the dog. I told Gene it was too cold in the house and I wanted to take a walk, get a bit of fresh air, but that was a laugh, or else it was a lie, because we all know that outside in Iowa in the middle of July the air is anything but fresh. The heat is soggy, heavy, thick with moisture and gnats and the constant hum of the cicadas, so loud and unforgiving that all you can do is let it grind into your brain and forget about it, if you want to keep from going insane.

By the time I'd realized my mistake, it was too late to turn back, because the little dog—a soft, sweet, spoiled mop with teeth—was already trotting down the walk, nose to the ground and surprisingly strong, forcing me to lurch along after him, in my sandals and sundress, as best I could.

The path at the end of the walk that crosses the grass behind Iris's house leads down to a creek, and it was encouragingly familiar to me. I have been there many times, sometimes with my mother and sometimes with my sisters, mostly back when I was just a little kid eagerly tagging after them, in all kinds of weather—out to pick raspberries or crunching through snow, shuffling through leaves, clopping in mud. That's what you do here, in the afternoon, after lunch or later, after dinner, in summer when the light is long.

But not then, it was too hot then, in the middle of the day, with the sun at its highest, the light at its brightest, the heat at its most relentless, when in my haste to get away from the terrible confinement of my sister's house, I didn't think to bring a hat, so there I was, exposed. I might have made it quick, an outing in gesture only, but then, what? Back to the house, back to shivering in that Freon chill, because Iris was on fire in the darkened bedroom with the blanket tossed aside. She kept getting up to turn the thermostat down and down, colder and colder still, with Gene traipsing after her, wringing his hands and scolding: Stay in bed, Iris, please.

He fixed her lemonade and brought her ice and slices of cold watermelon, anything to make her more comfortable, anything to cool her down, while Iris tossed, delirious, and complained—I'm on fire—when there wasn't really any fever, only fear, as in the phone call, when she whispered to me: Daisy, come, please come. I'm dying. I'm afraid.

When the cicadas screeched to a stop, the way they'll do sometimes, all at once and altogether, then their sudden silence was worse even than what had been their steady drone, in those woods all overgrown and tangled wild with nettles that stung and thorns that scratched, so I had to fight to keep to the path while the little dog strained ahead toward what he must have known was the creek, pulling me along with such intensity that in a minute I'd opened my hand and let him go, leash and all.

He tore down the path, barking, and then he was gone. I peered into the trees and they seemed to part before me, revealing a glint of light, sun on metal or sun on glass, which I craned forward to understand and discovered to be some kind of a small house, a wood shack there atop the palisade on the far side of the creek, and the glint was a gleam in its eye as it seemed to be gazing back at me. Had it always been there? No, that didn't seem possible, because I would have noticed it before, I would have known it, I would have remembered it then, but it looked too old to be new. Ramshackle even. It seemed to be empty. Abandoned. Left to fall in on itself over time.

I was drawn to it by curiosity first, but also something else, something bigger, deeper. Opportunity, it seemed. Or possibility. Promise, maybe. A sense that there was some meaning there, and in my current situation, with my sister dying, and my own rushed return to what had at one time been my home.

I considered leaving the dog to its own devices, turning around and heading up the path again without him, but what if he didn't come back? I knew well enough that they would already be expecting that sort of irresponsible behavior from me, all their suppositions and beliefs about me reconfirmed. They would be thinking: Isn't that just like Daisy to be careless at a time like this, to bring more work and worry to us, creating further hubbub, trying to be helpful and only making it all that much worse. Iris in bed, Gene hovering helplessly, Rose taking care of business, and Daisy, the fuckup. Mother said: 'Twas ever thus.

All along the dog had been barking, but then it stopped, suddenly, its racket snapped off mid-yip. I pictured him fallen, injured, cornered, a meal in the mouth of some larger, smarter, more ferocious animal, but if that was so, I figured—and might later be obliged to explain—it was not my fault but his, because after all he ran away from me on his own choice. I took one last glance over at the glimmer of that little shack between the trees and decided to thwart expectation by recovering the dog and bringing it back to them unharmed.

The path was muddier but less overgrown as I moved closer to the creek, which was shallow there and swift. I'd thought I might find the dog nosing along the shore, but he was nowhere in sight. I called to him, after taking a moment to think and recollect his name. Spike, Gene had told me, laughing, tickled—he had a boyish giggle that I'd found attractive, once upon a time. Iris had only winced, suffering, in pain. And Rose had stood in the doorway watching, while Spike hopped up onto the bed and turned a circle or two before curling close to his mistress, from which position he'd eyed us all balefully, daring anyone to send him away, with a low growl and a flash of teeth that said, clearly: Fuck off. At this, Iris had managed to smile.

I called to him again. There were bug bites on my arms and scratches on my legs. My skin once was fair and my limbs have always been long and lean, like stems, and that combination made of me a flower—this is an old self-image, which at one time may have brought to mind a vigorous sort of beauty, but there I was then, bruised, wilting in the heat, soft, frail, fading as my petals fell.

The dog bounded out of the trees. Filthy, panting, it seemed to grin at me. Its leash was gone, and the collar, too, and they'd all have something to say about that, but at least I had the dog, safe and sound. I scolded him as I gathered him up into my arms as if I were his rescuer. He squirmed, then settled, leaving a splatter of mud on my dress, a smudge of dirt on my cheek.

As I walked back up the path, I could feel that little shack behind me, watching me, it seemed. I turned quickly, stopped to look, to catch again the glint, but it was no longer visible from where I stood. I was thinking what a good person I was—there, doing that, for my sister—and the mud, the dirt, it was a sign of all my good intentions, so I smudged it up and made it worse. I wanted them to find me just like that, so I could say, See? I'm not perfect. I'm also a mess, like you.

I sat on the porch with the dog after dinner, both of us bathed and brushed by then, and me into my second glass of wine. I had the whole bottle to myself, because these folks don't drink, and they consider the fact that I do just another of my many weaknesses—knowing how Daddy was, and how Mother stayed away from it herself. Not that it did her any good. Or Iris either, it seems.

I would have lit a cigarette then, too, if I'd dared, but I didn't. The dog was asleep, there on the floor at my feet, exhausted from his romp. Rose was in the kitchen, cleaning up the dinner mess, and Gene was in the bedroom with Iris, watching over her, making sure she was comfortable and helping her with her meds.

I couldn't stop thinking about that little shack out there in the woods. I'd asked Rose about it, but she didn't seem to know what I was talking about and neither did Gene. Both of them looked at me with blank faces, ever so patient and ever so kind, as they waited for me to finish so they could go back to what they'd been doing, which was what? I had no idea.

If Mother were there, I thought, if Daddy were alive—I could have asked them, and they'd have told me, they'd have known.

I poured myself another glass of wine as darkness folded down over the lawn, the woods, the creek, the world all around.

Then Rose was in the doorway, her bag over her shoulder, come to say good night, good bye, she'd be back again in the morning. She invited me to go home with her, but I declined and immediately recognized the relief on my sister's face when I did.

Rose is the oldest of Daddy's flowers and I am the youngest, most beloved of all, which I've always felt I deserved because I was the prettiest and I was the happiest. Mother called me Sunshine; I was a glint of light there at the edge of Rose's lumbering shadow and beyond Iris's pure invisibility.

A while later, with Iris asleep, drugged and resting comfortably at last, Gene replaced Rose, looking at me the way he always has and wondering, should he join me or should he just go to bed, get some rest. Torn, he couldn't decide, and I didn't bother to help him, only smiled as he struggled with himself. Then I went ahead and lit the cigarette, smoked, waited, heard him sigh. He said, Good night, Daisy. I smiled, watched him turn, watched him retreat from me, slump-shouldered drag-foot. The burden of his life, of Iris's death, it weighed on him. While the little dog dreamed, tearing through the woods, and his deluded legs twitched. One yip, and then he yipped again.

Gene has fixed up the guestroom for me, with clean sheets on the bed, a towel on the chair, even a flower in the vase on the table, which Iris must have instructed, a peony from the garden. The quilt is one that Mother made. Iris was the one to acquire all the old things, including the house, because she has always been more interested in the material world than either Rose or me, and here in her house everything has been placed just so, on display museum-wise.

When I close my eyes, the room shifts and turns, a warm soft wine spin, and I am inside the wood shack, but it isn't ramshackle, it's new and it's clean, the windows are open, the curtains are blowing, and there is a smell of fresh paint, a gleam of polished floors. The furniture is simple and spare. This is my house, I know, it is all mine. My loneliness feels like freedom here. My solitude feels like home.

THE MOST TERRIBLE THING

Whatever it was, it wasn't good. There were the roses. And the guests. And a rainstorm drove them all away. Thunder pounded the air, smashing it like glass; lightning cracked the sky. The next morning there were snail tracks on the rocks, shimmering like magic; I told William they were fairy trails.

I know I had a son, a boy. I think there was a boy. It doesn't matter. I can't remember. I never can remember this. Not for sure anyway. But wasn't there a boy?

I'm on my way out for the flowers that I will put in the glass basket on the table by the door. We'll have guests tonight.

His name was William. Will, Willie, Billy, Bill. My mind spins a web: his memory clouds and clings and numbs and kills. He was my son. My only boy. My baby, my beloved. His hair was curly, and his eyes were blue.

"Jane," they said, speaking up, their faces close, "you have a son."

My body was an empty basket, hollowed out and still. I was shivering, flushed in a freezing sweat. Blood whispered and pooled into the mattress and through, onto the rug on the floor.

You almost died, they told me later, smiling, serving soup. Charles came and he held my hand. When was this? I can't be sure.

I walk through the gardens. My feet are small in satin flats. I am out to cut the roses; the gloves on my hands are soiled, smudged with dirt. The clippers are rusty and stiff. My hands ache. My dress drags behind me in the grass.

The boy was naughty. He disobeyed. He didn't listen. He was a bother. He never could keep still.

Herbs for the meat grow wild on mounds beneath the windows of the summer house. I've come out here to snip parsley, dill, tarragon, and thyme. The heat is conscious and oppressive; it bears down. Charles was expecting rain, he said. We kept hearing thunder. He said bad weather will always make the guests come late.

I can hear two people talking. Murmuring in the summer house, they come out to sit in the iron chairs, under the umbrellas in the garden, their long arms folded, their slim legs crossed. The heat bears down, a weight, a shawl. Ice chimes in crystal glasses. Lemonade and tea.

"Darling," he is saying. Her earrings glint a message coded by the sunshine.

She has her head buried in a newspaper. "It was on a cross-country flight. A birth in the bathroom. She was a teenager, they said. The father was from Georgia. My God."

He is cracking the ice between his teeth. She shivers and kicks off her shoes.

My baby's name was William. He was older. In a yellow slicker, running up the drive, across the grass.

Calling to me: "Mommy! Mommy!"

This was the first day of school, and his lunch pail was swinging, banging against his legs, bruising them, purple flowers blooming on the pale surface of his skin. He stopped when he saw that Charles was behind me, in the kitchen.

It wasn't William's fault. No matter what Charles thought. "You can't always be sticking up for him like that. He has to learn. A boy must be taught. He'll thank us for it later. You'll see."

Those two linger in the sun. Her head is cradled in his lap; his head is tilted back. Eyes closed, they doze. She dreams; he snores. Her mouth is open, saliva gathers, spills over, a rivulet down her chin. They don't notice me, walking by, my arms full of flowers.

The roses nod, heavy with the dew. A cat hisses, arches up, claws the air.

There it is again, that sound. Whack! Whack!

I don't remember these two. What are they doing here, in my house?

She says his name, leans in closer to him. She hooks her hair behind an ear. She rubs his shoulders. He closes his eyes.

Charles was thundering but little William wouldn't stop. He couldn't help it. His breath was hitched with sobs.

The most terrible thing. I had the roses in my arms. Glass, like ice, glinting in the pile of the carpeting by the door.

He was only trying to help. I told Charles, "He was trying to be good. Come now."

I pulled William away. There were bruises blooming thumbprints on his arms. Charles stepped in the glass on the floor, and it sliced through the bottom of his shoe, into the heel of his foot. He left behind a trail of blood that followed him through the house, up the stairs, down the hall, like the slime of a snail, like bread crumbs in the forest, footprints in the snow.

When asked about the blood, I told our guests that Charles had cut his foot.

This woman is in my kitchen now; she's standing at the sink with her hands in soapy water. She leans on the counter; she watches the window; she looks out at the sky.

"I heard her again last night," she tells him. She doesn't look over her shoulder, but I notice that he rolls his eyes. He looks at his hands and shakes his head. He thinks, sometimes, she's crazy, though to her face and to her friends he is always careful to say high-strung.

He's wondering whether it's going to rain.

The roses in the crystal basket nod.

"William!?" Where did he go? He can be naughty; sometimes he hides.

He went down for his nap, and never got up. The bruises left tracks across his back. The blood on his temple was slimy and warm; it bloomed on the pillow-case like roses on snow.

Wee William is sleeping in. His blood like a finger painting on the sheets.

"This house is haunted," the woman says. She shivers in his arms.

I am arranging the roses in the crystal basket on the table near the door. I am humming. It's hot. We'll have tarragon chicken and cold strawberry soup. Charles stands on the balcony and watches for the storm.

"The thunder," he says, "has a way of making the company come late."

MOUSE WARS

This isn't even a house, strictly speaking. It's just an old rundown shack in the woods on the creek, passed down from father to son to son to me. A getaway from the feminine constraints of duty and decorum, a place where a man could be a man, my dad said, having heard this from his dad who had heard it from his dad first. Play cards. Fish. Hunt. Drink. The jolly old camaraderie of all that. I held onto it more out of laziness than anything else, never guessing that Jimmy's change of heart would one day provide me with the privilege of calling this place my home.

The land around here once was wild and vast, but now they've taken down most of the trees and cleared the brush all the way down to the creek to build a tract of new homes there. Real houses, those are, meant for husbands and wives with jobs and cars and kids. Before the money dried up, that is. Before the builders called it quits. Now it's just another half-ass tract gone bust in the real estate balloon.

Consolation: it's not just me, on these hard times.

I have this one room; that's all. Kitchen at one end, cot at the other, dining set in the center, chair backed up beneath the window beside a standing lamp. Toilet tucked behind a curtain, along with a single shower stall. Booze in the cupboard. Shotgun in the corner. Pantry stocked with food. Plus an unmatched array of glasses and dishes, pots and pans, flatware and utensils, all swiped from other kitchens or picked up at garage sales. Everything you could need or want and none of it costing me a cent except the water and the power and the firewood I'll use to heat the place come fall.

He didn't think I'd have all this. He figured I'd go to a motel. Or a homeless shelter. Or the street. He'd have liked that all right, seeing me shivering on some corner one morning on his usual bustle around town in that little car we bought just before he put his foot down. Saying I was lazy. Calling me a liar.

He didn't figure on the shack or the cash or the credit cards and the bank account. He never reckoned I'd have seen it coming and been prepared. Didn't expect I'd find a way to look after my own interests at least as well as he was looking after his. Just waited for that last unforgivable infraction so he could file the papers and change the locks and call it all my fault.

My first night here, I was feeling the full freedom of the situation. Me letting go of him and he of me so then it was just myself and the dog and nobody to say yes or no or maybe, maybe not. Simplicity, all right. Silence too. Peace, at last. I was thinking I could find God that way, maybe, and how about that.

Bottom of the bottle and I was asleep and dreaming something complicated, with passages and caves and crawling around in the dark, but it was a sound that brought me to again. Thought at first it was a prowler. Gripping the bottle by the neck and raising it up in case I had to defend myself. The dog didn't even notice. She's old and deaf and, sure, he let me have her because she was already mine anyway. A nuisance, he said, letting her out the back door. Leaving her there in the yard, in the rain, with the gate open, and it was as if he wanted her to run away.

They took out the trees to make way for those new houses, so what were woods now are fields and that accounts for the mice. Not one or two, but a full-out infestation. And not just me, but everybody. A record year for vermin, they say. Everybody has them, fancy house and simple shack alike.

I listened to the skitter all night. A squeak. The rustle of cellophane, paper, tiny teeth gnawing through wood or nut or seed.

And now this morning, in the light of day, there was the evidence, which must have been there all along except I didn't notice. Cracker crumbs on the counter. Mouse droppings. A hole spilling kibble from its bag. I'd left the dirty dishes in the sink. Why? Because I can, though that was always more Jimmy's style.

He hoped I'd get sick. Something fast and brutal and then I'd be gone and it wouldn't be his fault. Didn't happen that way. Sorry. I'm not the sickly kind. My dad lived to be eighty-five, and then it was not disease, but the shotgun that got him. He made his own choices.

I've picked up seven traps at the hardware store. Along with supplies. More whiskey. Crackers. Cans of soup. After my dad passed, my mother lived on frozen food, and that was good enough for her. A microwave and a balanced meal in a plastic tray. The women in the family are stronger, that's just another trait, and Jimmy should have figured it before he said I do. Whose mistake was it then? His or mine?

These are the cartoon-type traps—wood and metal, red lettering stenciled on, and peanut butter for bait—though they also tried to sell me a new contraption that I hadn't seen before. No less inhumane, it's got a baited glue-pad. Simple concept: the mouse is hungry, he steps in, he gets stuck, then rips out his own guts trying to get away. You can let him die like that or just toss the whole thing into a bucket of water so he drowns. One way or another, the job gets done.

I passed on that thing. Baited the others; snapped my thumb and howled. The dog snooped around the peanut butter, but backed away like she knew it wasn't meant for her.

Another night and again there was the scurry and the creep, punctuated this time by the snapping of the traps; while on the floor beside my cot, the dog dreamed on, unaware. Seven traps, six snaps that echoed like bomb-bursts in the stillness of the shack. So quiet, I could hear the rush of the highway, miles off, like someone's sweetheart whispering in my ear. Music came and went too, faintly. From the development, most likely, where you can imagine wayward kids are up to no good together in the empty rooms of those half-built homes.

I had to wait for that last trap to go. On edge for it and my thumb throbbing, until intoxication overcame and I drifted off into a dream where a bear was waiting for me in the full-bloom woods, with Jimmy there beside him in his underwear. His muscles never looked like that. His hair is gray, not black. His bare feet glistened in the grass. Then came that one final percussion. With the bear barking and my husband lifted up into the air, so poof, just like that he was gone.

In the morning: seven traps, six dead mice. The live one had dragged himself off into a corner to hide. It took a while to find him there—one leg caught, the rest of him pulled in tight—he was pretending to be dead. I carried him down to the creek and hurled him high, trap and all. Watched him touch down in the dirt on the far side, near a wanton pile of boards. Admired the skeletal silhouette of a partially framed house, collapsed against the sunrise in the early morning sky.

I gathered up the other traps and had to spend some time working out how to let the dead mice go without any physical contact. Their little heads smashed flat. Not much blood, and that was a relief. One had taken a fully body snap that must have crushed its back. Greedy bastard. The smell of peanut butter turns my stomach now. I had to make a choice, decide which was worse: putting my hands in a pair of old gardening gloves or the feel of a dead mouse against bare skin. My thumb was turning black.

In my mind's eye Jimmy rolls his eyes and shoulders me aside to do the dirty work himself. Dog shit, vomit, baby mess. The time the cat was hit by a car and came limping home, its hind leg broke in half. I've never had the stomach for any such as that.

I was swallowing hard as I opened the traps and dropped the dead into a Ziploc bag. Sealed it, then held it up to see what seemed like a true accomplishment, which inspired an unexpected sort of pride. I longed for a chance to show the bag to Jimmy. Seemed like evidence of something. So there.

I showed it to the dog instead. Unimpressed, she merely blinked. Pulled herself up, hobbled to the door, and waited there until I let her go outside.

Two more nights of this, and that was about as much as I could take. Eighteen dead mice from the six traps. This was not a problem; it was a plague. Another trip into town to use the phone to call an exterminator, and I picked up some more supplies as long as I was there.

The dog slept on as the man banged on the door. With his fist, like this was a mansion, and maybe I didn't hear him from my chair at the table in the kitchen that was the living room that was also the bedroom. When he stepped inside he was big enough to fill the whole place, it seemed. I am not a large woman myself, and Jimmy was just regular size, so we fit together pretty well. Or so I thought.

It didn't take the exterminator long to figure out what was what. The evidence was clear—droppings, chewed papers, crumbs, and whatnot. They were coming in through cracks in the foundation, he said, or by way of the gaps around the windows and the doors. Following the pipes up from below perhaps.

All the while, he eyed me with some curiosity. Smelled my fear, no doubt. Or recognized my squeamishness, which made him smile. "Not afraid of a mouse, are you hon?" The name on the pocket of his shirt: George. An ape with hairy arms and his jaw already shadowing blue by early afternoon. I just smiled like it was nothing, turned away, busied myself at the sink and the view out the window at the half-built houses over there.

He kept on talking, to my back, telling me what I already knew. "Vermin. They're everywhere. Especially in a place like this." I turned to see he was looking around, taking it in—my cot, my chair, the table, the lamp, the bottles, the shotgun, the books—and when he looked at me again, it was like he thought he was on to something.

He said I'd have to seal up all the openings, but keep using the traps in the meantime. Glue-pads, too, that he would provide. I had to sign a waiver for the poison, in its black metal box in the yard. "It'll kill that dog, you know. She won't get into it, will she?" "No," I told him. "Not a chance. No."

The mice will be drawn to it though. Then they'll just go off elsewhere to do their dying there. A mile at least, maybe more.

At night the development is dark. No power in the

empty houses and no moon in an overcast sky, so the shadows are thick. A flashlight beam cracks through them, now and then. Those kids are out there prowling around. Throwing rocks, shattering glass. The dog lifts her head, barks once, then drops chin to paws again. I lie on the cot, listening to all this, my sense of hearing heightened. Added to it is the rustle of the mice and the syncopated snap of traps. Overall, it feels like a solution of some kind, even if it's only temporary.

You can make a bad choice and not even know it until you've gone so far down the line, it's impossible to trace back from one event to the next to find the starting point. Where did it go wrong, you ask. Or wail. Or whisper. Pour another glass and sit at the table because you can't sleep while the mice are out there gobbling up poison or struggling on a glue-pad, tearing themselves to pieces in their efforts to get free. While the dog snores and the night is so black and the shotgun in the corner that once belonged to your daddy seems to be calling a special kind of attention to itself.

Jimmy didn't even cheat on me. That's how sure he was. When he saw my surprise, he shook his head. "What did you think was going to happen?" he asked. Did I assume we'd just go on like that forever? There was no other woman. Or man, even. Just…he'd had enough and he wanted me out. He's there in our house now, on his own because that's how he wants it and he knows I will do anything for him, including leave him alone, if that's what he needs, and even this makes him despise me all the more. What do you want from me? I asked, trying to find some hint of something in his eyes.

Dad said, "You need to know when it's time to take your leave of things. Get out graceful." My mother said, "Just try not to leave a mess behind for someone else to have to clean up once you're gone."

In the morning the traps were all full again. I did the disposal routine—plastic bag, gloves, plus a mask that was really just an old ski cap with holes cut out, pulled down all the way to my chin. Like a superhero, I thought, recalling how I'd tied a towel to my shoulders when I was a kid and got myself to believe that was all it was going to take for me to be able to fly, not reasoning further: If I could do it that easy, then why wasn't everybody else doing it too?

I was ruminating on this and opening the traps—emptying them one by one into the plastic bag and trying not to look at those glue-pads, just dropping them into the pail of water—when a car pulled up onto the grass behind my own. Even before she opened the door, I knew it was Sil, come to rescue me. My sister is younger, but she's larger than me and she was big as a kid, too, which made her early years bad enough that she grew up to be a woman even larger and with a greater presence, you might say. A barking laugh and broad gestures and clothes that scream on her.

She had on some big dress all full of flowers, with a purse and sunglasses and some kind of strappy shoes that made her look like one of those cartoon hippos dancing on tiptoe. Her face was red from the heat and the struggle she had getting out of the car.

The dog looked up from whatever it was she was doing and squinted at my sister. Tail moving cautiously. Sil stopped abruptly. Took a fright before I pulled the cap back to show my face, and then all she had to say was, "Honey, what the hell?"

I was quick then, with the last of the traps and the glue-pads and the bucket. There was one brave fellow with his hip smashed, and he was swimming desperate circles. Sil was coming up the steps, and I was pulling off the gloves, solemn and trying to make it look like this was nothing. *Hi*, I said. She was beside me, peering into the bucket, and so together we watched that one mouse still paddling through the bobbing others, with their eyes popped and their little skulls crushed and their vivid innards turned inside out.

All I could think to say to her was the obvious: "Mice."

Sil took it upon herself to clean the shack then. Hanta virus, she said. People were dying in Yosemite. Sweating. Her big bare arms flopping around and the dress getting caught up between her legs. She took off her shoes and left them on the porch, then slapped around the place, barefoot like a peasant. She was doing me a favor, she thought. Or said. Or maybe that's what I was thinking. I didn't say it. Dishes first. And sweeping. There was no vacuum cleaner there, so she was bending over the dust pan, then dumping its contents in the bin. She checked the doors and told me what I already knew, that I was going to have to seal them. She left and came back shortly with duct tape and wood putty and this foam she squirted into the cracks. A runner for the bottom of the door. The tape was for the windows.

I went out into the yard for this. Sat in a chair in the shade and dozed there. Listened to Sil moving around inside, sealing it all up for me, just so. There was also the hollering of the kids in the tract, busy with some game. And the dog at my feet, too, her chin on her paws, eyes open and alert—she was watching my every move.

When the job is done, Sil comes out onto the porch, her arms full of her supplies. She huffs down the steps and across the yard to her car. A can of Comet drops and rolls and spills powder on the grass, near the poison box. A dying mouse hunkers nearby. I nudge it away, out of sight, with my foot.

Sil is flushed, red-faced, damp with sweat. Glowing. Smiling. She hugs me. Engulfs me in her swamp and then pulls back. "You'll be fine," she tells me. Like she's thanking me instead of the other way around. And I know that next thing she's going to start bringing friends by. Inviting me for dinner at her house. Matching me up with this one or that.

"I'll come back to check on you," she says. Pats the dog, whose tail wags doubtfully.

When I go inside, the cabin is clean and fresh. Damp. Shining. The sunlight comes in through the window, sealed now with duct tape. The glasses in the cupboard gleam. The bed is made. Even the tip of the toilet paper has been folded into a little triangle, as in a hotel.

I make a little mess. Throw some things around a bit. The dog, on the rug, scratches and turns, before she settles in.

Saturday night, then, and I'd go out if I had anyplace to go. The development is quiet. Things will stir up there later, after the kids have fueled themselves with their girlfriends, their sticky fingers, and their beer. But now, it's quiet. And dark enough that you could almost picture the woods still there, feel it in the open timbers of the half-built homes. No moon again and clouds, so there is no light and nothing to see. I'm sitting on the porch. The mice are gone, it seems. The dog sits beside me, attentive, and together we watch the darkness. I think about calling the exterminator again. Maybe thank him. Maybe ask him to come on by and check the traps.

ALL THE TIME

~~~~~~

The wheelchair at the top of the steps is a good safe distance back, and the brake is on. They checked it more than once before they left her there to watch them walk down the drive to where their car waits in the parking lot beyond—a glitter ball of chrome and glass under the high sun of midsummer, midday. Their backs retreat, their faces are hidden from her now, and their figures are vague, but for a splash of color. The blond hair, his green shirt, the girls' bare legs, their mother's red shoes.

She holds the little dog in her lap. Gummy eyes, hanging tongue, panting grin. On the other side of the steps an old man sits on a bench, his shoulders hunched and his hands twisted into a burl on his knee. He'll sit like that for another hour, sweating, until a nurse comes to take him back inside where it's cool. He knuckles a cigarette. They can't make him stop smoking; nobody even bothers with it anymore. His lungs are already ruined, along with the rest of it.

She doesn't look at him, but watches the family as they are absorbed into the glint. The dog pants, shaking her. Her hand on him is dead weight, useless, fingers spasmed into a claw. Her mouth droops on that same side too. Sag in her cheek and the one eye half shut. Monstrous, she thinks, and avoids reflections. She peers at the mirage of the parking lot and opens her mouth. A moan at first. Clucking tongue. Then the moan again. The dog watches her, flexed, ready to leap away. Her hand on his back presses down, holding him in place. She groans now. Grunts. Clears her throat. The struggle further twists her.

The smoking man glances her way. The two of them flank the steps like gateposts. Smoke emanates, steams up around him, silently. The sky is bright, relentless. She moans again, then lifts her good hand, raises it high above her head, the way they've taught her to do in therapy. She holds it there, a gesture, a signal, a word made flesh, moving slowly back and forth: Good-bye.

It's as if he's done it on purpose, but that can't be. Alice is in the front seat and the girls are in the back, each against her window, both hoping to catch a draft from the air-conditioning. She didn't see what he was about to do until it was done. After they'd followed the long swoop of the drive to its end—or its beginning, depending on how you want to see it—where it meets the road that was to take them back to the highway and then to the interstate and then to the city and finally home. A Sunday visit to see his mother is all it was. The girls along for the ride, and that's a rarity now, to have them both, without the extra encumbrance of boyfriend and husband and kids.

The woods on either side of the drive are thick and full, a midsummer tangle that brings to mind memories of childhood play. Forest magic, peculiar creatures, abandoned tots, lovers rolling around beneath the trees. Except these woods are not that dense and they're not that expansive. Just a bit of green border sheltering the Home—as it's called, sometimes fondly, sometimes not—from the world.

Alice put on her sunglasses, sat back, and watched the asphalt roll out before her, toward the gate at the end. Or the beginning. Home, the real home, is less than an hour away. She'll take off her shoes and change into shorts, then pick flowers from the garden for the tables in the house.

Walter pulled to a stop at the end of the drive. Ann, in the backseat, coughed. Sally said, not for the first time, She looks good, I think. Reassuring herself, or them.

A tractor lumbered by. Walter had to wait for it. The GPS piped up, in her calm voice, and told him to turn left. He watched the tractor pass. A farmer was perched on the seat, his sleeves rolled up, one hand on the wheel, the other on his knee. The broad brim of a seed cap shaded his face and sunglasses hid his eyes, so it was hard to tell: old man or young?

The asphalt ended, the gates opened, another car was waiting to turn in. Walter had pulled forward. He hesitated, and then he went right. Ann moaned. Sally said, quietly, Dad. The GPS recalculated, and Alice turned to look at him. He kept his eyes on the road, then nodded in agreement. Yes, he said, she looks fine. His mother. Then, I know what I'm doing, he added, eyes still on the road.

She will not flinch at this. Alice will not rise, though the girls in the backseat have already started to complain. She holds steady, her own sunglasses hiding her own eyes as well as the sting in them, which she quickly blinks away. She has nowhere to be, nothing to do, all the time in the world. If he wants to go another way, that will be fine with her. He says something to the girls, glances at his wife. She notices that his grip on the wheel has tightened and feels the car jolt forward as he speeds up, kicking gravel.

Apparently he knows of a detour that in the long run will be faster than being stuck behind that tractor. This way is prettier, besides. The scenic route, he says, smiling into the rearview mirror but catching no one's eye.

Alice rolls down her window and the car is filled with the smell of fresh-cut grass. A rush of air ruffles her hair; a caress.

Sally has sunk into a sulk. Her face turned aside, she must resign herself to this day with her parents. Soon enough she'll be able to tear away from them. This is a girl who lives in her head. You never know what she's thinking, but the suspicion is that it's the opposite of whatever she says or does.

Ann is still complaining. To Alice the rising pitch of her older daughter's voice has always been an irritation, and she knows what Ann means even though she can't quite catch the words, and also that this is a pose, though for whom it isn't clear. Ann has left the babies at home with their father and she wants to insist that she must get back, she doesn't have all day—when really this should be a relief, to be out and on her own for a few hours. If she could only let go. Alice doesn't have to turn around to know what Ann looks like: puffed up, heavy, her small eyes, her hair cut short, haphazard, without care. Everything she does now is aimed toward convenience. She'll be reaching for her purse and the bag of candy there, to suck on the comfort of something sweet.

Alice will not rise. She will not flinch. But then she does, rolling up the window again first, then turning to her husband. She wants to tell him: It will be all right if you change your mind. Turn around and go back, the right way, the way we came, the way we know. He's upset about his mother, Alice understands that—he's always upset about her, whether he visits her or not, and he can't see how that plays out in what he says and what he does, afterward. Clinging to a past, a memory that isn't even true, was never a reality, but has since shifted and become so in his mind, ever since the starburst in the old woman's brain that left her as she is now. Alice would like to find the words to comfort him, but even before she can begin he's turned to her, and his face is distorted by what he means to be a smile, but it comes off as something else entirely. A snarl. I'm awake, he says, insisting. I know what I'm doing.

It's true that sometimes he dozes as he drives. His eyes close, lids drop, sometimes. She's seen it, and she watches him, but he always denies it. She's keeping her own voice low—she doesn't want to bring an argument into the small space of this car. We're not in a hurry, she says—meaning he can follow the tractor and it will turn off eventually, probably soon—but he nods. Exactly. We have all the time in the world. And looking in the rearview mirror, trying again to catch the eyes of the girls, he goes on: It will be an adventure. And: A little change of pace never hurt anybody.

The GPS is telling him to turn around. He ignores it, and it recalculates. The scenery on either side slips past. The girls are talking to each other now, just low enough that Alice can't quite hear, and she supposes they must know this, that they do it on purpose, always have. The car has been divided. Parents, children; front seat, backseat. As if without knowing it Alice has somehow taken sides and she and Walter are in it together, deciding where they'll go next.

She reaches up, pushes back her hair, rests her head, turns off her hearing aid, and sinks into the silence with a sigh.

Walter has made the right choice; he's sure of it. That tractor would have slowed them down, impossible to get around it on this narrow road that curves onward through the woods. They'd have been stuck behind a farmer in a hat, wasting gas all the way to the interstate, and then the girls would have been arguing about that instead. Urging him to pass or warning him not to. Like birds, pecking at him, which at least would help keep him alert maybe. Or maybe not, and anyway he knows how to stay awake on his own. Blinking. Whistling through his teeth. One hand on his knee, scratching through his pants. Plus he has the GPS if he needs it, so there's no way to get lost. It's too simple for that out here in the country where all roads lead to the city anyway, because they have no place else to go.

He thinks the girls should be happy. He thinks they should appreciate the scenery. He thinks they should appreciate everything more than they do. Taking him for granted, for example. Taking themselves for granted too. Everything. All of it. When this life could be ruined in a moment. One shining light of blood in the brain and then there you are in a wheelchair trying to say something that nobody understands, and nobody knows what you're talking about because you're not talking, you can't talk anymore, so nobody knows what you want or what you need, they just have to assume, they have to guess, though it's a demonstrated fact that Sally really is best at that. Listening to her grandmother and then passing on to the others what it is she's been trying to say. Except it's hard to know whether what she comes up with is right, or even close, but at least it's entertaining. Telling Ann: She wants you to put on a hat. Then going to the closet to get it and put it on her sister's head. Ann red, uncomfortable, her face flaming, greasy-looking as it is these days, some allergy or something—the babies, the extra weight—and Mom smiling at it, as if yes, that's exactly what she wants. Sally patting her hand, triumphant. See, we understand each other, you and me. She wants you to give me some money, Dad. See, she wants me to have what I want. But that was a joke, even though she had her hand out, and Alice scolded her for that. But Mom just kept smiling so maybe it wasn't a joke after all.

No appreciation for the beauty of this place. A summer day and what's their hurry? He knows the way. Sort of. The general direction at least. This road will hook up with the highway eventually, and then it's only a little bit of backtracking to get them where they would have been anyway, ahead of that tractor, which might have already turned off, but never mind, because the choice was made and here they are. Even the GPS has stopped correcting. Recalculated and figured Walter's detour into its grander scheme. He knows what he's doing. He scratches at his knee.

The girls were close as children, close in age, alike in personality it seemed. Two peas in a pod, their grandmother called them. The Peas, she said. How are my little Peas? Taking them into the house. Shooing Alice and Walter away, delighted to have the girls all to herself after bringing up a full family of boys.

Not so anymore: a glance in the rearview shows their separation. Bookends now to the empty space between them. Ann leaning against her door on one side and Sally against hers on the other. Ann with a book; Sally gazing out at the scenery. Maybe she's stoned. Walter wouldn't put it past her. On this scenic route that's just more of the same. Fields, woods, creek, farmhouse, old barn, new silo, car for sale with a price on the windshield. Yard full of junk.

As they get closer to the river the road begins to roll, rising and falling, and the scenery peters out into a cluster of houses and fences and trees. He finds it beautiful, the dapple of sunlight through the leaves. He's alert and feeling nicely energetic. This fine car. His fine family. He's carrying them, the four of them together, in a way that has lately become so rare, as the girls go on with their lives and their jobs and Alice is out doing whatever it is she does—volunteer work, mostly, and social things, book clubs, and workouts at the gym—which leaves him alone at home on his own a lot of the time.

Not that he minds.

The road makes a turn here, a sharp curve toward the water, and he takes it too fast, skidding on the gravel, which causes the girls to sit up and Alice to open her eyes in time to see the fallen tree that blocks the way. Sally yelps as Walter slams the car to a stop.

It takes Ann a moment to figure out what's happened. She can't see anything out the windshield but branches and leaves. And Sally is bleeding. Mom is turned around in her seat, trying to help and shouting because her hearing aid is off, while Dad has unhooked his seat belt and is getting out of the car. Ann puts her book down and shouts, Mom! Mom! Then reaches out and touches her. Grabs her and gestures—her ear. Mom stops. It's quiet for a moment as she reaches up to turn the thing on. Sally is out of the car now too, spitting blood from her bit tongue onto the dirt of the road. Mom follows. And, finally, Ann. Now the four of them are standing together, side by side, looking at the tree, the road, the car. The heat is oppressive, wet, and swarming with mosquitoes and gnats. Ann sweats. Her skin prickles into a rash at the back of her neck.

Dad is smiling sheepishly. He's apologetic. They can all jump on him now, he says, about driving this way, taking this route. At least he stayed awake. He lights a cigarette and stands, contemplating the road, the tree, the car.

"Hey, it's nothing," he says, "all right? It's fine. We'll just turn around and go back." He can admit that he was wrong. He can say he's sorry, that he made a mistake. Now the trip home will be twice as long, but at least they're okay. Ann steps forward to back him up. She should be the one who's angry, but she's not. It's nice to be here, with her family. She almost thought: her *real* family, as if the other—husband and babies— are something else. But anyway it's nice to be away from them, to be a child again, not really in charge or responsible for anything. She has given Sally a wet wipe from her purse, and she keeps an eye on her mother, who is looking at the fallen tree as if she can't figure out where it came from, as if it toppled just now, a near miss, this close to catastrophe.

Alice sits on the tree, in the shade among its leaves and branches, half hidden as if she isn't even there. Her deafness isolates her and she's lost in her own world, in her own head and hearing only her own thoughts. Or nothing at all.

Ann slaps at a mosquito. She tugs at her shorts, which are too tight and have ridden up her thighs; an intimate pinch. Her mother has turned away to watch a hawk circling the sky above them, over a field some- where beyond where they are now.

Sally has been leaning on the car, her arms folded. She's chewing gum and smiling at her sister as if they share a secret.

Dad puffs on his cigarette, squinting through the smoke, calculating what will be his maneuver, the rever- sal he's going to have to make here on this narrow road with shoulders that drop off sharply into the ditches on either side. There will be some turning and backing and turning again to get the car headed in the right direc- tion, but they can do it, and the girls will help; they'll guide him through it.

A wind picks up and rolls toward them. The hawk is gone. Not a cloud in the sky. The blazing sun. The fetid ditch. The tangled weeds and dark mud, swarming with flies. The wind rocks the trees then dips to catch Mom's skirt and lift it, revealing soft white thighs, varicose bruise, black lace panties. The wind twirls her; it sweeps through her hair. Ann is buffeted too. Sally yelps again.

The wind moves on, following its own path through the trees, and then the hawk is back and Mom is looking around, wondering whether anyone saw. Dad is stepping on his cigarette. He brushes his palms. All right. He turns toward the car. Let's do this.

First he had to back up, away from the tree. Ann took a position near the left front fender and Sally stood at the back, stepping away as he rolled slowly toward her. The Volvo looked like a large woman, big hips bouncing under her skirt of blue paint. Sally stumbled over a loose stone but caught herself, and the brake lights flashed. Walter was pulling forward then, turning toward Ann, who waved him on until he stopped and spun the wheel around the other way, then reversed again until the tires had crept onto the shoulder, nipping at the ditch reed before Sally put her hand up, fist clenched, to stop him again.

All of this is pantomime. Alice shades her eyes. Ann is waving at her father, drawing him toward her. Sally sneezes, then swipes her hair back from her face.

The car was perpendicular to the road and not an inch to spare. Alice opened the door and climbed in with her husband so that then it was just the two girls on the road, one on each side, at the lip of either deep ditch. Walter backed up again, rolled forward, back again and forward again, inching the car in a circle round the angle, until it was straight with the road once more.

Leo would survive his own life, which from day one—when his nervous young father dropped him on the floor—has been a rolling road of mishap and disaster; and it shows. Although experience tells him, too, that if he can find his smile he can also get some of his old (young) self back, if only for the moment, and if this particular girl isn't able to see it, at least he can feel it all right, lurking there just below the wrinkles and the creases of his weathered skin. Leo Spivak is never unaware of the dimple in his cheek, the sparkle in his eye, the crafty glint of gold tooth between his lips.

But if we look a little closer, we'll see that the dimple is actually a scar: dog bite. One thin worm of raised tissue circles halfway around his throat, and another, longer and more tangled, runs down the inside of his right arm from elbow to wrist: glass patio door. The spatter of an oil burn fans across his lower back: exploding lamp, and a thick white line crawls up the inside of his left leg: hidden nail. Like any old stray dog—nose scratched, ear torn—Leo Spivak has nicks and scars all over his body and a story to go with every one. He might be taken for a fighter, although that's not the case. Accident-prone, is how he likes to tell it, with his slanted smile, when a girl like this one gets around to asking him about the remnants of his wounds. Sounds sexy, in Leo's estimation. Has a tendency to make them guess him to be a daredevil of some kind. Not a good idea, though, to encourage that impression in the mind a girl who is about to climb into the basket of his balloon. And anyway, she hasn't asked, although if Leo has his way, there will come a time when she does.

This one, she's quiet. She hasn't shown much excitement or even curiosity, and she didn't thank him with more than a raised eyebrow when he took her hand and helped her climb aboard. There is something about her though, even looking so young as she does—

maybe because she's such a little bit of a thing—something in her eyes or in the set of her jaw, that makes Leo suppose she's seen enough to know better than to care or believe she might have any control over what happens to her in her life anymore.

There used to be a time when a girl like this one would find Leo Spivak attractive, drawn to what she'd be thinking must be his bad boy ways, a girl in search of some kind of punishment for herself. He doesn't get that reaction much anymore, though, unless the girl is drunk or high or the bar lights are dim enough to make her think she's looking at someone younger and greener than himself. Still, whatever else he's lost over the years, Leo Spivak does still have the smile. The dimple and the wink. Not to mention the hands—slim, long-fingered, delicate-looking in a way. And it usually comes as a nice surprise to a certain kind of woman, he knows, when she finds out that he's not the cruel man she at first guessed him to be. When he holds her and she comes apart in his arms. Used to be, anyway. Once upon a time. These poor messed up girls, worked over by somebody sometime, led to think they deserve to be damaged. Some things never change.

The roar of the burning propane makes conversation unnecessary, as the balloon rises up to catch an easterly drift, toward the prettiest vista to Leo's eye. Passing along the southernmost edge of Linwood—where you can just make out the silhouetted saints on Bohemie Bridge, the grain silos at the cereal plant, and the gleaming windows of the taller buildings downtown—the balloon floats on over the river, toward the deepening green of the early summer woods. From there it's easy to forget about the flooded creeks and storm-ravaged towns that scab the landscape all around and admire instead the occasional barn, falling in on itself with picture postcard perfection.

Leo closes the valve with a turn of his wrist, and they float on in simple silence. The girl still doesn't seem inclined to talk, and he won't push her. He's been at this job long enough to know when to become a part of the party and when it's better for him to hold back and become a part of the balloon.

She's dressed all in black—hooded sweatshirt, black jeans, faded and torn, black sneakers. She has her dark hair tied back with a black ribbon, and her face is pale, her chin thin, her mouth small, lips chapped and chewed. The only color on her is the pink in her cheeks and the green in her eyes. Her small hands clutch a black pouch. All along he's been assuming it holds a camera, and he's been expecting her at any minute to unzip it and start shooting.

Leo can see the dust from the chase truck below, rolling down the gravel road that circles out toward Highway 10, where the splayed fingers of the lake shimmer under the early morning sun. He's aiming for the high field past the woods on the near side of the water, just above the spill. He checks his watch, then fires up the propane again, and they rise a bit more. He looks to his passenger for a reaction but gets nothing. She's gazing out at the landscape, the pouch held close against her breast. For a second it looks like she might be crying, but maybe it's only the wind making her eyes gleam like that. Or maybe she's afraid. She doesn't seem like the timid type though, not when she called last night to book the flight or when she showed up at the crack of dawn this morning in a battered black Cougar with mud-spattered lightning bolts detailed on its back fenders.

And then it occurs to him—maybe she's a jumper. He's heard of them, never actually had one himself. He moves a step closer to her, bounces on the balls of his feet as she leans forward, out over the edge of the basket for a glimpse of the ground so far away below. Then she's swallowing her anguish by lifting her chin and closing her eyes against the brilliance of the sky. He puts a hand against her back, to steady her, and his fingers feel the hum of her muscles and her bones. When she takes a deep breath, opens her eyes, squares her shoulders, and unzips the pouch, he relaxes, steps back. It looks like she's just up here to take some pictures, after all. Maybe she's an artist. A student. Going for some Grant Wood kind of vision of her own. Moved to tears, overwhelmed by the beauty of the world, its awesome glory glimpsed from on high, and no wonder.

Leo runs his own gaze over the sensuous curves of the sunlit farmland below. Deep black dirt, plowed and ready for planting. He has closed his eyes now too, just for a moment, to absorb what he believes to be the girl's panic and inhale the loamy smell that wafts upward with the morning warmth. Which is why when he looks at the girl again, it's too late. She's already leaning out over the edge of the basket with both her hands outstretched. She's waving the pouch, shaking it briskly, creating a gray swarm of ash and bone that billows out, silvers in the sunlight, then scatters and is gone.

Ashes. A fucking funeral. He should have known. It all fits—the last minute booking, the cash payment, the phony name.

"That's illegal, you know," he says. "You need a permit."

She turns to face him. The basket rocks in reaction. She glares at him as she zips the pouch up shut again, folds it, tucks it into the pocket of her sweatshirt. She shows him her palms. Abracadabra, no pouch, no ashes, no crime. Her smile seems to be as slanted as Leo's own, and she's able to hold onto it for a moment of recognition before her shoulders start to shake. She gasps as if punched, her face breaks, and her eyes spill over with tears, until there is nothing for Leo to do about it except reach out, pull her close to his mangled body, and cradle her there as she falls apart in his arms.

THE LOST ART OF LISTENING

~~~~~~

The Moon Glow cottages were set back in the woods, back-dropped by a mountain vista with a drastic drop-off toward the road, and from the front porch—it wasn't really a porch, more like a stoop, four feet square with barely room for a chair—you could get the full vastness of the view, the sky wide and high and your own puny presence there amongst the chipmunks and the crows.

Sam was no one. He was nothing. She didn't love him. She didn't know that he loved her. Or if she did, she didn't care. They were friends, that was all.

He'd unpacked and put away his things, such as they were. The compact rental car gleamed in the glow of the yard light now that it was dusk, and its engine ticked. The other cottages were dark as far as he could see—which wasn't far—as they trailed off down the winding path farther off into the mystery of the trees.

"Yours has the best view," the old woman had said, handing him the keys. Her teeth were ragged in her smile. Her T-shirt was torn at the neck. Her boots were stones as she stomped off to her own house up the way. Neon in the night: "Moon Glow." "Vacancy."

The stars stared down, observing him with stunning unconcern.

The screaming started with the last beer. He'd

popped the top and slurped the foam. The starlight had begun to blur in a way that let him know that yes, he would get some sleep tonight. He'd settled in the chair on his stoop, bundled against the chill that seeped in from the shadows, from the trees. Bats had given up their swoop. The forest behind him was still. The silence had turned deep and cold.

At first he thought it was a cat, yowling. But then the shrieks widened, heightened, filled the air and the forest all around. A woman? Some violence being done to something. An owl's screech? Some sort of attack, predator and prey. A coyote with a rabbit, say. A mountain lion with a fox. Or just the rutting bugle of an elk, though spring isn't the season for that. One scream, high and mighty, and then two.

At the third, he was on his feet. Beer cans clattered off the porch onto the grass. The chair smacked back.

Sam was a coward. He was a chump. He was a drunk and lost and lovelorn fool.

The next morning he was up before dawn, as was his habit. Creeping around in the dark with the thrill of knowing the rest of the world around him might still be asleep and dreaming, but he'd got the jump, and by the time they were digging into their breakfast he'd have already put in half a day's work. As if that mattered. As if he'd make good use of the time as it stretched out into emptiness and ended up swimming in beer. Or worse.

It was the dissertation, piling up pages on "The Lost Art of Listening," which he'd been digging into for the last three years as if it were his own grave. Or so she said before she packed him up and sent him off to get the job done, once and for all. "And don't come back until it's finished," she said. Her hair a halo in the morning light. Eyes bright, smile wide. She loved him in her way, but not like that.

He slithered from his bed—it wasn't a bed; it was a cot—and stumbled to the bathroom. Didn't stumble, plodded. Slapped bare feet against bare wood as the mountain chill sifted in through the crannies and the cracks on the whistle of the wind.

A scurry of something—mice maybe. He looked out the window to see the night submerged in fog, with woodland gleaming through it—trees sentry to the horizon, marching up the gulch—and the surprise of lights in the beyond. Thick beams shafted upward from somewhere deep in the forest that rolled all the way up toward the tree-line, before it staggered and fell short.

He leaned closer to the glass as if that might help him see. Blinking. Squinting. Shivering at the sight of five lights beaming upward. One began to move to the left, slowly at first, then faster. It slid off to fade in the fog where the meadow opened up toward the road that fell away into the valley and a winding rill of runoff after that.

A second light moved left—to the east he figured—then dimmed and disappeared. The others shimmered, softened, faded, brightened, hardened, and again there were five. No stars. No black sky. Just a gauze of low clouds, hanging mist, and the lights.

He wanted to call out to someone and say, "Hey come here, look at this, what the hell is that?, Do you see it too?" She'd sit up, groggy, annoyed. She'd straggle over, pushing back her hair, nightdress falling open. Or no, T-shirt hanging slack. And then eyes widening, jaw dropping. "What *is* that?"

There was a family in the cottage next to Sam's. Not a family, just a woman and a kid. He had a glimpse of her. Face at the window. Flash of flowered fabric in the doorway. That cottage had a better porch, with an overhang for shade.

The kid was in the yard. Sam was in his doorway—mountain sunlight clear and clean, whispering pines, scurry of chipmunks, swoop of hawk, call of crow—waiting for another sighting of the mom. Fat, he guessed.

"Hey mister," the boy said.

Sam stepped down from the porch. The kid had been scratching figures in the dirt with a stick. He was a lumpy boy, with thick limbs and big feet, a flat face and eyes that squinted through thick glasses beneath a thick tangle of blond hair. Damaged, Sam supposed. Something missing upstairs.

Until: "Hey, mister. You see them lights last night?"

Sam was supposed to be working, but instead he was searching. He was supposed to be disconnected, that was the whole point of this place—Moon Glow—and him in it. She had set it all up for him. The price was right in the off-season, when the snow was melting up top, then draining down to sodden the land below. He had a typewriter and his books and his files. No laptop, no internet. Just Sam and his ideas and the pages piling up.

The kid—idiot or genius—turned circles in the grass. His mother sat on her porch, dressed now in big jeans and a T-shirt over bobbing breasts, gazing at the sky. Idiot or genius herself, it was impossible to tell. They might have been thinking the same of Sam over there on his stoop, poking at his phone, peering at its small screen.

Aurora borealis: "A natural light display in the sky particularly in the high caused by the collision of energetic charged particles with atoms in the high altitude atmosphere." But that featureless glow didn't match these lights, which had shone straight up, like spot-lights. And these lights had moved.

Now the kid was rolling in the mud and the mother clapped and laughed and showed a mouth full of broken teeth when she turned to grin at Sam, her blond hair crazy on her head. He waved and smiled back. The kid was a pig in the muck.

Maybe it was something to do with the fog. Distorting lights on the road that wound through the valley below the crest, say.

Or hunters with flares or lights, moving through the trees, but it wasn't the season for that.

What else?

Aliens?

She would have said this first, he knew. So he called her.

"Hey." And, "Hey." And, "What?" And, "How's it going?" And this and that until he finally came around to the lights, and then she lasered right in and said, "Are you working?" And, "Yes, sure, of course. I'm just taking a break. There's this retarded kid and his mother here." He figured she'd find that funny, because that's how it used to be. Her phrase: "You're a magnet for crazy people." Which was supposed to be an asset, but now it had become a flaw. "Takes one to know one," like that. So off she went, and it was as if she had a right to her cold appraisal. Big sister. "You loser, Sam. You'll find anything, use anything, to keep from doing what you need to do. An idiot and his mother? You're corroborating with them about some lights in the sky that you think you saw? "She sputtered. Her outrage bloomed until she couldn't go on. That's how much she disliked him anymore. She slammed the phone down. Or anyway the connection was lost. The planets turned. Stars wheeled.

The kid was naked in the yard, squealing as his mother hosed him down. The old lady in her boots was busy pulling weeds along the drive.

The mom stomped through the grass and up onto Sam's stoop. She banged on his door, shocking him up out of the depths of his investigation—UFO sightings now, and what they meant. Extraterrestrials or glimpses into a deeper reality? Outer space or inner space and a bald man with glasses telling him to have no fear—so that by the time he opened the door she'd spun herself into a storm that blew the knob out of his hand and slammed him back inside.

It was something about her son and how he'd scared him. Sam looked past her to the cabin there where the boy sat curled in on himself and thought, didn't say: "Not me, ma'am, you scared him, you're scaring me, I've got work to do, I don't have time for this, you and your retard kid."

The old lady had come to her door then, too, and she was glaring at the two of them, hands on her hips, flowered cotton dress, varicose shins.

The mom stopped. She took a breath, pulled herself up, and threw her shoulders back, causing her breasts to lift in an appealing way. Her hands were in her hair. It occurred to Sam then, that her life must be very difficult. A woman alone. With a moron for a kid. Or whatever it was that was wrong with him. Maybe it swung the other way and he was a savant. Autistic, like. Maybe he played the piano, songs he'd never heard. Or counted in prime numbers. Calculated calendars forward and backward in time.

"I'm sorry," Sam said. Keeping his eyes on hers— which were a surprisingly brilliant green—Sam stepped back, two paces. Her hair seemed to glow in the sunlight. Her cheek was bruised and her mouth was slightly open, pink and moist, revealing that feral gleam of ruined teeth.

Two steps back. A nod. And then, slowly, carefully, gently, he closed the door.

He waited until he was alone. Staring at the wall, the floor, the small print painting of a field, green with grass, bright with some kind of yellow flower that didn't seem real.

The mother and the boy had gone rattling off in an old truck. Hillbillies, he decided. There was something wrong there, besides her looks and his dim wit. Maybe she'd stolen him from somewhere—a mall, a school, his father—but why not a better kid if you were going to go to the trouble of that? And then the loop: because if the kid was stolen and he was smart, he'd tell, so she'd had to take an idiot and make him hers to keep. Too dumb to know the difference, like.

He shut it off right there and got up and got going. He wasn't sure why it mattered that they'd gone, except he didn't want questions or comments or conversation or explanations or expectations. The old lady's place was dark, too. He guessed it was siesta time with the TV and a beer and the fan on high. The sky was so bright and blue it was like a migraine up there waiting to descend and swallow Sam whole.

Behind his cabin there was a path that dipped down into the gully, between the trees and then wound along its way, getting colder in the shadows. It was wet, too, so maybe there was a creek down there. A stream anyway. Runoff from the snowy peaks, feeding the river full of fish, the reservoir, the city down the way. All those toilets flushing, then off toward the sea. The intricate connections between things killed him sometimes.

He was looking for evidence, but what kind? Burned turf. Broken trees. Flare remains. Evidence of fire. Or boots tromping. Pressed grasses, crop circles.

Was it as simple as a gang of school kids in the woods for a party? There was evidence of that: bottles and cans and rubbers and butts.

The stillness scared him. The woods, pristine and ancient, seemed primeval, as if no one else had been there since the beginning of time. He felt there must be predators around, hidden just out of sight, following him with yellow eyes. Animal or alien or human. Such thoughts stopped him in his tracks. He could feel the crawl of eyes, that shiver of attention, that buzz of contact, his skin was singing with it. "You're not alone, son," his father said, meaning something else altogether. Where were the birds? Where was the wind? The stillness was so deep it felt like death.

Except Sam's own clomping around as he shook free and moved on, tearing through the brush and stomping on the path, coins jangling in his pockets—if there was anything out there it would hear him coming and would flee or hide. Critters anyway. Hunters, maybe not, and in his white shirt and brown shorts he didn't want anybody guessing he was anything but a human and not a target or the meat for their next meal, animal or man or alien, any one of them.

He had a talent for whistling that was useful for parties and drunken walks back home from the bars in the city after dark. It was good for the girls, too, if there were any. For some reason they seemed drawn to a man who could whistle a tune. Good lips, maybe. Good tongue. Gap-tooth man, whistling goat, twinkle in his eye.

Ultimately she got sick of it though. Another charm that had become an irritation. "Shut the fuck up," and all that. Because he was always putting pop tunes in her head, and she couldn't shake them out again. Now, one his own, hands in his pockets jangling change and a whistle in the air—"Take me home, country road," or somesuch nonsense, with variations in the trills—he was strolling in the woods like a regular gentleman farmer. Like he owned the place. And expecting to find what?

Footprints, huge and ragged in the mud. Bigfoot? A yeti with a flashlight. A whole gang of them with a whole bag full of flashlights.

Or burned spots. Scorched earth. Tinny patters of tiny feet. Little grey men hunkered in the bush or looking down on him from the tops of the trees.

Boys with headlamps and guns out hunting coyotes and deer.

What he found instead was blackened trees and broken glass. The glitter of it stopped him in his tracks. His whistle was cut short and the tune was left to hang. There was the screech of a jay. Skitter and squeak of chipmunks. Marmot bark. Crow swoop. Hawk's slow turn.

A little ways beyond a stream flowed past, pretty as a picture book, and on its other side a cabin, all dressed up in *No Trespassing* signs and tangles of barbed wire, was busy falling in on itself, an implosion of logs on a weedy hump of land. "Violators will be prosecuted. Hunting on private land is prohibited by law."

The water looked too wide and deep to cross, and anyway Sam had seen enough. He crunched back through the broken glass, past the blackened trees that yielded to the green glory riot of sudden spring. Bursts of yellow dandelion. Wildflowers of every color waving in the breeze.

None of which explained the lights Sam had seen out there that way the night before.

The mom was hanging clothes on a line and the kid was inside doing who knows what. Equations, maybe. Poetry. His little pants and shirts flopped in the breeze. Her skirt tangled in her legs.

Sam sat on his stoop throwing back a beer or two or so. Sips of bourbon in between. He examined his legs—the bloody scrapes and scratches evidence of some battle he'd won, because after all, here he was. Until the old woman came tromping over—in her boots and her T-shirt and her tits flopping and her yellow hair like chicken fluff—to tell him not to leave his empties in the grass. Just the sight of her drove him back inside again. That and the mom glaring at him like he was doing something wrong by just being there in the world at the same time as her.

He tried to read, but couldn't do it. He closed his eyes and was gone to another place, until he woke to the last dusk and dry mouth and fuddled head. He warmed a can of beans, then sat at the table shoveling them in with his fork held awkward, throwing back the bourbon to wash them down.

A vigil at the window then. He set himself up just so. Chair. Binoculars. Bottle.. The kid had stopped his caterwaul and must have been sleeping. Sam pictured the mom, curled on her own bed. Snug. Fan turning, sifting a breeze in her hair. Cooling the sweat on her throat.

That was far as he chose to take it.

He was at the window, looking out the other way, facing the forest and waiting for the lights. To him they were a sign that there is more to it than what's already here, more beyond all this, more than just him. More than only her.

Long past dawn and the heat of the day was already settling down on the world, pressing, full of flying things—mosquitoes, bees, butterflies, hawks and crows and screaming jays. If there were lights in the night, he'd missed them. Snoring at the window, forehead on the sill. He pulled his hair down forward to hide the indentation when he saw the mom and asked her if the boy had seen them again. She said nothing, only looked at him, then turned away, the anger coming off her in waves so strong he almost reached for her, to touch her, put his arms around the storm and hold it close against himself, feel it rage.

So then he couldn't ask the kid either.

The old woman was out sweeping the walks. Flaccid butt under baggy shorts.

The sunlight moved across the floor. The typewriter was still. His cellphone was dead. "This is what you wanted," he heard her say. She'd kick him if she could. Like kicking a motor to cough it into life. Or a dog to get it to stand up. Or a door to get it unstuck. Fly open. Walk through.

Sam will try to see the lights again tonight. And then again tomorrow. He'll be watching, waiting, for as long as it takes.

A coyote howls on the rise above the Moon Glow cottages, chasing rabbits through the dusky meadow off beyond. The rill spills between its rocks. Crows scab the trees. Jays scream. Woodpeckers knock. A mouse shudders in the high grass.

In the yard, the child runs and squeals. His mother lights a cigarette. Smoke roils; she smiles. The old woman, on her knees in the dirt, leans back, lifts her face to the sun, closes her eyes.

All this, he thinks.

She told him. She said: "Sam, it has to be enough."

DAWN

Maybe it's true what they say, that accidents happen more often to people who live alone. Maybe there's a clumsiness that sets in, as you climb up out of your body and into your head. No one is there with you but the dog, the cat, the bird. A telemarketer on the phone. The television in the kitchen. The radio by the bed. You speak to all of them, but you're really only talking to yourself.

Because it was winter, I didn't go out much. I was all set: pantry, freezer, fridge all stocked with food.

More than once it crossed my mind that I should move, find something smaller, with less space to rattle around in. Something simpler than that house that felt like it belonged to someone else. Once my mother's, now mine.

I'd cleaned it out, room by room, and lately only occupied some small space at the back. The upper story was mostly boarded up, to save on electricity and gas, and the extra rooms downstairs were closed off, too. My sister had moved to Arizona where it was warm, and she'd encouraged me to visit. Please come and *see* us, my sister wrote. She didn't mean come and *stay*.

I'd spent Christmas alone, because I was stubborn and frugal and couldn't see the point of trying to get from one place to another at the busiest and most expensive travel time of the year. Plus I thought the gifts would have to be more extravagant when offered up in person. So I'd held my ground and made excuses. I had obligations at the church, I explained. Something with the choir. Which was a bold-faced lie because I'd quit that months ago, after an argument that I couldn't even remember anymore, what it was about. Some slight, some sting that had seemed untenable at the time, but soon had faded into meaninglessness. I'd only joined up anyway because Mother said I should.

When I went upstairs, it was bitter cold, and I should have bundled up. There'd been a storm the night before and the streets were snow-packed. I'd have to shovel the front walk if I wanted to go out for any reason, which I didn't. I thought I'd rather just keep to the kitchen, dozing in the La-Z-Boy, near the stove. Reading my mysteries. Watching my shows. Talking to the dog and listening to the bird singing in her cage. I could make a stew, which would last me all week. I also had my knitting. Baby blankets and preemie caps—my good deeds, my contribution to the world beyond my own four walls.

So I could have stayed put and been fine, but there was the closet at the back of the house, in the room that had been mine when I was a girl, living with my parents and my sister and no inkling that this was where I'd eventually end up.

A carton on a shelf in the closet, that was all, with a newspaper clipping and a name that I could not for the life of me recall. It was right there on the tip of my tongue, but that was as far as it got.

You expect there to be more harm in winter. Slick sidewalks. Snowy roads. Shorter days and darker nights. Gas heat. All around more opportunity for an accident to happen, even if you stay inside, mostly, and are alone, mostly, and don't go out into it—the bitter cold—for days on end because you've stocked up and you have everything you need and you have no place to go anyway, because you quit the choir and your family has diminished—father gone, mother passed, sister moved away to someplace warm—and you lost your job when the old man you'd been caring for went into a home and died.

I am a cautious person. I wasn't lonely, and yet the solitude that winter caused me to sink into myself, and so for a moment my mind was elsewhere. I wasn't looking. I wasn't paying attention. And statistics show that accidents happen frequently to women who live alone.

I shivered in the cold. I didn't dally, but went straight to the back where the windows overlooked the woods behind the house. There was what had been my childhood room, where for years I'd slept, secure, and there was the closet, with its rattle of empty hangers from a cleaners long gone out of business, and there was the carton, just as I'd left it on the shelf.

I carried it carefully, in both hands. I was deep in thought, remembering something about school and riding my bike and losing the money I'd been given to pay for something extra. I recalled my mother's dismay. My father's fury. It was money that I've worked ever after to make up.

As I made my way back down my view of the steps was blocked by the carton, and when I thought I was at the bottom, I stepped out toward the floor, but I'd miscalculated and there was nothing but thin air. My foot curled under first and then my full weight, plus that of the carton, came down on it, and I fell with a sound so loud it rattled the house and knocked snow off the roof. It seemed to shake the whole neighborhood, I thought, as I lay there and felt my foot begin to swell.

The carton was overturned beside me, with its contents spilling out, and I remembered it then, the girl's name. Not Dorothy or Barbara, it was Dawn. Dawn. The name gonged in my head.

This was exactly the kind of accident that can kill you. A woman alone in a house falls down the stairs and no one knows. She's broken her leg or hit her head, and it's days and days before she's found. Weeks. Months. By then she's starved to death. Papers pile up on the porch. Mail fills the box.

Except my leg wasn't broken, and I hadn't hit my head. I could stand all right, but any weight on the foot brought excruciating pain. I hobbled into the kitchen. I left the carton behind. I thought I might pour ice into a bowl or use a bag of frozen peas, but I had neither ice nor peas, so I hopped over to the door and stepped outside and stood barefoot in the snow until I couldn't take it anymore.

Eventually the swelling went down, but there was a magnificent bruise that turned my foot into an eggplant at the end of my leg, already distressingly varicose beneath my robe. I couldn't get into a proper shoe, so I wore a colorful sock. I used a broomstick to get around, limping from sink to fridge to table to stove and back again. I slept right there in the La-Z-Boy that first night, tilted back with the foot propped up. An x-ray was out of the question. I wouldn't be able to drive, not with only one good foot and not in the treacherous snow. I could have taken a cab to the hospital, but that would be a waste of both money and time, because there's not much you can do for a broken foot anyway, except give it a rest.

I felt the fall all over again, whenever I closed my eyes. Stepping into the air, toes first, and then my foot folded under and the rest of me crumpled down on top of it.

Eventually I was able to bring the carton into the kitchen and spread its contents out on the table. A yellow ribbon: third place in a horse show. Snapshots of people I didn't recognize. Report cards. A plastic ring. Whose stuff is this? I wondered, so far now from who I'd been then, a girl who collected things like barrettes in the shape of butterflies and a pink rattail comb.

My hair had been long, braided every morning and brushed out every night. This was my mother's obsession, not mine. Her own hair was thin and short, and it sat on her head like the fuzz of a baby chick, yellowy from her smoking in the kitchen with the windows shut. My father sat at the table waiting for his food to be served. He drank whiskey before dinner and beer while he ate and then more whiskey after. The radio was on, playing out a baseball game. The dog was whining on the porch. My sister was off somewhere with a friend. I took a knife and sawed off the braids, one after the other, then coldly watched my mother weep. My father held them up—to me they looked like pieces of myself—then he threw them in the trash, and later I felt the horror in that, too.

This was around the time of the assault, just before Dawn and her family moved away. A time when I was mad at everybody, always. For a while I tried to change my name to Dawn, but it didn't stick.

The clipping wasn't there. It had somehow been misplaced. But anyway I wondered if maybe I could try to find Dawn again. I looked in the phone book first, thinking she might have come back here to live. Maybe she even had a house right down the street. Wouldn't that be something? I thought it would make a good story: two women, old chums, reunited again after so many years apart. We'd have a lot of catching up to do.

I was also trying to remember, if I ever knew, where she'd gone. Chicago? Minneapolis? Detroit? But probably Dawn's name had been changed anyway. If she married, say. The boy that we both had a crush on, say. That Tracy Travis, the dreamboat with the blue eyes and what seemed to be the kind of name a movie star would have, or a musician. Dawn Travis, then, but there was no listing for that, either.

There was a Dale Travis, though, and that was Tracy's brother, who I supposed must therefore be out of jail.

I called him, but got an automated answering machine, impersonal, not even a name, just the number, and "Not available." I didn't leave a message. What would I say?

"Hi, my name is Dawn."

Dawn had said it made her feel alive, what Dale and Travis did to her. She told me, she liked it. Her hands taped and her mouth taped. It became her story, and she'd tell it to anyone who would listen, which after a while was nobody but me, who remained in thrall to it to the end.

While Dale was in jail, the story grew. His own parents had given up on him after what he'd done, not just to Dawn but also to himself, and to them. The dad used to beat him, it was said, and some, my sister included, assumed that was why. The kid was too smart, Mr. Travis told the court, and so maybe he'd had to knock his son around to make him stupid.

It was snowing again. I didn't turn on the TV. I just sat there in my kitchen, and felt the throbbing in my foot, like it was a sign I was still alive.

Dawn tried to keep in touch with Dale, afterward. She wanted to know how he was, and could she visit him? And could she write to him? But Dale wouldn't have anything to do with her.

Dawn's feelings were hurt. Her heart was broken. She didn't understand. "Why not?"

It was a long time before I tried calling him a second time, because for a while I forgot all about it, the way you do. Things come up and life goes on. The foot was better, though I still limped a bit and now I used a cane to help me get around. I'd soaked it in Epsom salts while I sat at the kitchen table playing solitaire, only getting up to put the dog out, then let him back in again. It seems like the whole winter went that way, until it was spring, which doesn't last long in this part of the country where it will go straight from winter into summer, where one day it's still cold and blowing and then the next day the sun's there, and the humidity with it, and you have to call the man to take the storms down and put up the screens and then it's lawnmowers and sprinklers and kids out of school on bikes or in the woods, up to no good. The same kind of no good me and Dawn and our friends were up to back in our own day, only worse.

Dale still didn't answer this time either, but anyway I didn't hang up when the message played. I gave Dawn's name, and then there was a pause, with my hand in midair and maybe his, too, and then his voice, asking "What do you want?" And I said, "Is this Dale?" and he said, "You know it is. You called me, didn't you?" He didn't ask, "Is this Dawn?" because I'd already told him it was.

"Long time, no see," he said.

I agreed.

"You still in town then?"

I told him, no, I was in Arizona. Then, "I found you in the phone book. I was thinking about you this morning. Wondering what ever happened to you."

"Curiosity killed the cat," he said.

"Okay," I said. Maybe so.

Dawn had told me: "I never felt so alive as that, you know?" She was in love with him because of it, it seemed. "The way he looked at me," she said. "Like I was real, for the first time. Nobody ever looks at me that way," she said. Like when a bird flies into the glass and sits there for a while, staring at you, stunned, Dawn was tied up and watching Dale. He had the gun, so he took the brunt of it because he was old enough, but Travis was younger and so he could go all juvenile and insist that he was only following orders. The DA and the judge agreed to just give him enough time to get the psychiatric underway, and who knows what happened to him after that.

"I'm coming in to town," I said. "Family business," I explained. And, "Maybe we could meet."

Dale was quiet at first, and then he said, "Why would we want to do that?" When I didn't answer, he said, "Maybe."

I said, "Next weekend."

He said, "Okay." He'd probably be around.

Could be he was curious, too. Or what Dawn had described, maybe he'd felt it just like she did and so they had that between them.

There's a park downtown where old men play chess and moms push strollers and businessmen eat lunch. There's a fountain, and I said, "I'll meet you there." In the morning, eleven o'clock, on a weekday, before the lunchers came.

I wasn't sure whether I'd recognize him anymore. He had long hair and brown eyes back then. He wore a headband, Indian-style, and an army jacket over torn jeans. I figured all that had probably changed. Not the eyes, maybe but now he'd be bald. Most likely fat, too.

I was at the park by nine a.m.. I wanted to establish my presence there before he showed up.

And what was he imagining he'd find? Dawn as he remembered her? With her blond hair and her long legs, in a miniskirt and tall boots? Smoking a cigarette, looking over her shoulder at him? Or bound and gagged, her eyes wide with fear? "Don't hurt me," she said she said.

A cop came by and looked at me, but he didn't really see me and he didn't stop to ask why I was there. I had my knitting to keep me busy. I wasn't bothering anyone.

I thought it was likely that Dale wouldn't come, and I began to plan what I would do next, but then there he was. I would have known him anywhere. Jeans. T-shirt. Leather jacket. Sneakers on his feet. Not bald. Not fat. He strolled through the park like he owned the place and didn't give a glance to me. A cup of coffee in his hand. Sunglasses. He was looking around for Dawn. He took a seat on a bench under a tree, in the shade. He checked his watch. Lit a cigarette. Sipped his coffee. Eyed a mother by the fountain, with a child holding a balloon. She didn't look at him, so he knew she wasn't Dawn.

He scanned the park, then checked his watch again. Irritation twitched in his face. Like he had better things to do. Like he didn't want to be played the fool.

He stood. He threw the cup away. He took one last look around the park and then, finally, his eyes fell on me. He saw me looking at him. He noticed the knitting in my lap. I was no Dawn, never had been, never would be, but still.

The child began to scream when the string left his hand and the balloon floated off. Dale and I both turned to see it go. I observed the fury of the boy and the desperation of the mother, as she tried to calm him, but there was nothing she could do to make things right again. That balloon just floated on upwards and away. It was one of those shiny metal ones, glinting in the sun, higher and higher, as it went, until it was only a speck, and then it was gone.

When I looked again, Dale was gone, too, and there was only me, an older woman on her own, at risk in the world, waiting for the calamity to come.

WHAT SHE DIDN'T DO

~~~~~~

What she did: went to see a movie alone, in the middle of the day, in the middle of the week. She left school and rode the bus downtown. She was fifteen years old. This was sometime in the spring and it was not warm yet, so she had a coat. A poncho, to be exact. And boots and a hat and gloves. Black tights. A sweater. Short skirt. Her hair was short then, too—mod-style. She pierced her ears because sometimes people thought she was a boy, which wasn't very observant of them. An old woman, a clerk in a department store, peered at her and asked, "What can I do for you, young man?" which shocked her, though she didn't protest. She was wearing jeans then. And a sweatshirt. She had been looking at toys.

A movie theater was a dangerous place, according to her mother. Nowhere for a girl to go alone, the likely refuge of men with nothing better to do with their time, men who were there for a reason and not a good one. Probably not to see a show. For example, her own father never went to movies. He watched the news on the television in the comfort of his own home and read the papers and listened to music, mostly classical, sometimes jazz. Stories were not for him unless they happened to be true. The made-up kind were for children and women, and so by that reasoning any man who was in a movie theater in the middle of the day in the middle of the week must be up to something else. And any girl who would put herself in such a vulnerable position in the company of such a man was just asking for it.

She can no longer recall what the movie was, or why she felt she had to see it. *Alfie* or *Blowup* or *Fahrenheit 451*. She sat in the back row, supposing that would be safer. Closer to the exit and no one could come at her from behind, though the place was mostly empty anyway. Just a few women, in fact, up near the front. Secretaries on a break or some such thing as that. Plus the man in the big coat, who sat in the same row, a few seats away.

The lights dimmed, the movie played, then somehow he was beside her. His arm was on the back of her seat. She kept her eyes on the screen. Saw flashes of color, but stopped trying to follow what was happening there. Pretty soon she was kissing him. Or he was kissing her. He kept his hands to himself. It was only his mouth, that was all. It felt good. He was gentle. He smelled nice. She never really saw his face. If they talked, she doesn't recall what was said. Maybe he asked her name. Maybe she lied and said it was Petula because at that time she wished it was. When the movie was over, he went away and left her blinking in the light until another man came in to sweep. That one didn't look at her twice.

This is just something she remembers, and even then only vaguely. It doesn't mean anything to her. It says nothing about her. It was a mistake to mention it to her husband. That only added fuel to his fire, the way he already suspects she has a secret self. Sometimes she catches him looking at her with this expression of doubt. He peers at her, trying to see past what he can observe, to something else, something he can't know but anyway is certain must be there. Like a nugget of some truth buried in the fluff of the lie that is her appearance. She's pretty. Everybody says so. He would like to tear her open to get a good look at it, that nugget, and sometimes he does just that, but in the end there's nothing to see.

They've been married for forty years, and lately it's been getting worse. He tries to trip her up. She's out for a walk and sees his car idling at the end of the block. He pretends he's not himself. She walks right up and slaps the window and he turns, slowly, to look at her. Doesn't even bother to make up a story. Doesn't say anything at all. Just pulls away, goes home, where she'll find him later, at his desk, trolling the internet for information because he's working on a story that he knows nothing about.

"What were you doing out there?" she asks, but he brushes her off. He's busy; he can't be bothered. And anyway he knows she knows and she knows he knows, so what's the point of talking about it?

He's pretty sure she's up to something though. He makes up a scenario: She's off meeting a lover, maybe a man, maybe even a woman. Someone younger, many years younger, say, a student maybe. Or a colleague. Or... anybody, it doesn't matter who.

He's been at this sort of thing for as long as they've been together and at first she found it flattering that he would think she could do such a thing. That she might be attracted. That she might be attractive. "I've seen the way they look at you. You don't know what men are like. You don't know what they can do."

This was at the start, when they were younger. He doesn't say that sort of thing anymore. Because no one looks at her anymore? Or because she does know now what men can do? Still, it continues to be a game with him and a habit and she supposes he keeps it up because it makes him happy.

He calls her when she's out to lunch with a friend

or at a meeting or an appointment or running errands. He calls her to see if she'll pick up, to see if he's interrupting anything important. He'll have a small request for her, something so flimsily concocted: Could you pick up this or that? What was the name of the___? When will you be home? If she doesn't answer, he calls again. Or sends a string of texts. Her phone buzzes madly in her purse. It's his way of saying, "I know you."

This time it isn't the usual argument, the one they often have when she gets home and maybe he's been drinking if it's evening or he's been napping if it's day. Groggy, either way.

She's been at the vet. The dog is twelve years old and hasn't been eating. It's suffered other ailments along the way, too, but this time she's had to leave it behind, overnight, for observation.

Never mind that it's raining. Or that the garage door won't open again, so she has to run from the driveway to the front door with her bags and it's locked and he's at the TV—turned up loud because his hearing is gone—so he doesn't come until she's banged and banged. Then he wobbles out into the hall, looming there, peering at her through the glass as if he has no idea who she is.

By the time she's in and has shaken off her coat and toweled her hair and put the groceries away and dinner in the oven and poured a glass of wine and smoked a cigarette in the empty garage and kicked the door and fiddled with the button to no effect—by then he's ready for her. The news is over; a game show bongs in the background. Her head throbs. The phone rings, and she takes the call. "Your dog is resting comfortably." A reassurance from the vet's office, from a woman who is maybe too wrapped up in the animals— the heavy girl in pink who works at the desk and seems to think they're the ones who pay the bills.

When she hangs up and reaches for her glass, he's there, staring at her. "Who was that?" She tells him; he doesn't believe her. He smiles. "Clever," he says. And, "You weren't here when I got home." Sniffing her, trying to kiss her, as if it were a test. Touching her hand to measure its warmth, and she knows what he's thinking and also what he wants her to say, which is something like, "Don't be silly," or, "No, I never," or, "Don't start that again, please." Instead she says nothing at all.

He asks about the day. Where did she go? What did she do? And when? He tries to trip her up. "But didn't you say…?" And so on, until she stops and looks at him, lets the silence unsettle him, then turns away. She goes into the kitchen. She shuts down the oven. She pours another glass of wine. Comes back into the living room where he sits with his hands clenched and his jaw clenched, and she wants to say to him, "Yes. It's true. I'm sorry. His name is ___. He works at ___. I met him ___ . We've been___."

He will ask questions then, and she'll answer and whatever she tells him, he'll believe. "Yes," she doesn't say. "You were right. I did do that."

What she didn't do: sixteen years old and away at school because her father felt she'd put herself in danger falling in love with a blue-eyed boy who was a year younger and lived in another part of town. She went to his house after school and they rolled around on his mother's bed, kissing, touching. He was the first boy to see her without clothes and there was thrill enough in that. They didn't take it as far as they might have, but somehow her father knew and he "removed her from the situation. For her own good." He and her mother conspired. They packed her up and by fall she was away, safe, they thought, among other girls, behind an iron fence and a locked gate, in boarding school.

On Saturdays a bus took the girls into the city and let them go. She had friends, but she preferred to be alone. She liked to walk. She was on a path in the park, and a man on a bench had spotted her. She was wearing the necklace that her mother sent, a souvenir from a foreign country where her parents vacationed while she was away. It's only recently that she's begun to wonder whether that was the real reason she was sent off, so they could be free of her. The house without her and her anger, it must have been a wonderful relief to them. Though her mother always insisted that she missed her terribly.

It was a silver coin on a silver chain, shining on a young girl's chest. She imagines that the glint of it was what caught his eye. A girl skipping down the path. A man planted on a bench, eyeing her. Dazzled, maybe. She stopped when she saw him. His smile was bright. He was amused. He seemed old, but probably he wasn't. Maybe thirty. In a suit. A businessman of some kind, she supposed. With a warm tint to his skin. Dark hair, slick, groomed. She had time to notice his green eyes. He smiled and asked her name. Invited her to sit with him. Took the coin in his hand, between finger and thumb, delicately, and examined it. "From Corinth," he said. And then examined her. "My home," he said. "That is, my father's home. We come from there." His nails were perfectly manicured, which she had not seen in a man before. He wore a gold ring with a black stone in it. He touched her hair and listened while she told him about the school and the dormitory and the rules. Not mentioning the boy with the blue eyes. He said he would call her. An older couple was approaching, holding hands. He looked at his watch and stood and walked away, quickly. His groomed hair gleaming. The coin on her throat warm from his touch or her skin or the sun.

He did call. He had a plan. He'd come by the school for her. He'd say he was a family friend. Or an uncle. They could have a day together. She'd be free to do whatever she wanted to do. She only had to request permission. Next Saturday. That soon.

What might have been, in the end was not. She said no. She only went so far, and then she backed away.

She tries to make her husband see that what she didn't do is more important now than anything she did, but he isn't interested. He'd rather know about what he thinks she did. He wants her to tell him all about it, whatever it is. He wants to show that he was right, that he's been right about her all along, all that he's imagined for her, that it's true.

She drives to the vet to pick up the dog, and he follows her in his car.

She's begun to think there's no story to her life, because nothing of any real consequence has ever happened to her. She has a friend whose husband is in jail. Another whose child has died. She has no children of her own, and she wonders if maybe that's something that's happened to her, by not happening to her.

She has begun to see the empty spaces in between. The silences where she didn't reply. The look she didn't return. The touch she shrugged off or avoided altogether. The call she didn't take. A man invited her to join him for lunch and when she understood what he was asking, what he really wanted, she declined. He'd been misled because she smiled at him. Because she sat next to him at a dinner party and because she kissed him goodnight afterward. She was drunk. She kissed everybody. But he thought it meant something.

Her husband is so sure she has something to hide. Her face heats up. Her hair changes color. An "A" appears on her chest.

She puts on her boots, her hat, her gloves, her coat, to take the dog out for a walk in the woods behind the house, where they have acres and acres of land that her husband inherited from his father. A creek runs through it. The house sits on a bluff. The dog romps after the squirrels. The sun is mean in the sky. She knows he won't follow her here.

When she gets back he's standing in the yard, in his shirtsleeves and his shorts. He's holding a letter, as if it's evidence. He's been in her room. He's been in her desk, her drawers, her papers.

His face is livid. The dog barks at him as if he were a stranger threatening her. Bares its teeth, snarls. He tries to kick it. She moves toward him. Takes the letter and lets it go. It lifts upon the wind like a bird and the dog goes after it, tearing back across the yard toward the creek.

She lets the wind toss her around a bit as she staggers through the woods. Branches waving. The path a tangle. The dog long gone. She can't stay out here forever. Even the animals know better. She imagines the dog has crossed the creek and followed the trail to the houses over there. It's done that before. Someone will see it. Someone will take it in, but not to the pound, she hopes, though it's a sweet dog and pretty and someone else would surely come along and see it and choose it, give it a good home. With children. And a nice yard. Fenced.

By the time she gets back the storm has passed. The house is dark. The garage door is shut so she can't tell, but she's guessing, maybe hoping, he's gone. She lets herself in through the front, afraid at first that he will have locked her out, but he's done no such thing. She finds him sitting in the kitchen. His hands around a cup of tea. Like a child, he seems, his eyes wide, imploring.

She takes off her coat, lets it drop on the floor. She steps out of her boots, which are soaked. Lifts her skirt to pull off her stockings. He watches this. She turns up the heat and shakes out her hair. Then she sits across from him.

"It's been going on for a while," she says. "I'm sorry. I'm bad. I won't blame you if you want to leave."

He wants to know more. "Who is he?" She shrugs. Sits back. "I met him downtown. He gave me a lift. A chance encounter, that's all it was. It isn't anything. It means nothing. It's over. I'll stop." She licks her lips. "Where?" he asks. "We took rooms," she says. "Different places. Once we went all the way to ___ and stayed there overnight." "Is he married too?" "Yes. But she's a pig. Fat, you know. He doesn't love her." "Does he love you?" She shrugs. "Don't know. Probably. But it doesn't matter. It's over." "Have there been others?" She pins him with a look, sharp. "Do you really want to know?" She sees him flinch.

She takes a deep breath. Spreads her hands on the table. Looks out the window, through the lace curtains, at the trees, still now. She listens for the dog. The cat on the refrigerator regards her, waiting, too. Wanting to know.

He stares at her. "Yes, I do," he says. "Tell me. Were there?"

Slowly she nods. And answers, "Yes."

THE BEGINNING OF THE END OF ALL THAT

~~~~~~

I will say nothing about what I know. When John comes in, emanating winter in his wool coat and his scarf and his cheeks rosy, his nose bright, his eyes, as always, like ice. If I didn't know it yesterday, then I will still not know it today. By the time I see my husband again, I'll have already put it all out of my mind. And he can continue to rest assured.

What I know is what I've always known. What I don't know is, who sent the note. There was no postage, so I have to assume it was hand delivered. Someone walked it to the box. Or drove it there. We can't see the road from the house, because the driveway is almost a quarter mile long, and when we bought this house all those years ago, one of the things I loved about it most was exactly that, our remove. Then, there was a white fence—now that's gone—and, for me, an attraction to, a sense of fortitude in, the idea of that daily half-mile walk to pick up the mail. Also gone. Or in sending the children for it, later, when there were children. There were none. With the dogs alongside, romping. Chasing each other. Chasing a tossed ball. Yes, over the years, there has always been a dog.

You're a romantic, John said, and that was a part of what he had found attractive about me, then. But now here we are, and time has passed, and romance doesn't last. It hardens with knowledge, with experience, it turns to rock, then erodes to dust, then blows away when you're not looking, leaving a hollow cave, an empty place, all dug out, where the dreams used to be. Things are as they are, not as we might wish them to be.

Dr. Valentine shakes her head. She purses her lips. Frowns. Even on the radio you can hear her frown. Cut the crap, she says. Her phrase, this is, her catchphrase. Cut the crap. I have the T-shirt and a mug and a set of Post-it notes to remind me of this. Cut the crap. If you can just do that, she says, you can do anything.

The long driveway, the mailbox, the dogs, the white fence, even the children. That's the crap needs cutting. To get to the point, which is this: a white envelope. A yellow card, folded. Blue ink. "Your husband is a liar." A photograph. John's face. His hair. His hands. An entanglement of limbs. It's hard to tell which is which. Or who is who. But what's what is very clear.

It didn't have to be this way. It could have turned out altogether otherwise. You make one decision and then that takes you to another and then after a while you get to be a certain age, my age, ours, and it happens. You look back and you look around and you wonder about what you've done. Sure, everybody knows this is so. But maybe what you didn't expect— maybe even worse—is that you're seeing what you didn't do. I'm guessing that when the word gets out, no one is going to be much surprised to know what John has been up to all this time. Although they'll love to talk to each other about it. Some will be glad to see it ruin him. Our friends have wondered, I know, it's obvious—what can he see in a wife like me. He, so handsome, so important, so charming, so strong. And me, the sky, the greenery, the grass. I'm the background space, something for him to stand out against. You keep me grounded. His words. He used to tell me this. So be it. I am the ground upon which he walks. I'm the rock, and he's the wind. He changes, he goes here and there, but I stay put, and I remain the same. And all the while, we both, together, age.

So no surprise then, really. They must have supposed he's been up to something. Whatever it may be. Which I have chosen not to know.

Last night I dreamed of Henry Beale, the boy that was one of the choices I didn't make. Because I had found John, or he had found me, and I told Henry, simply, it's over. I handled it badly, I know that now, and maybe I knew it then too. His pale face, smooth and hard. Jaw clenching. Teeth bared, as if he might be about to bite.

No, that's not right. The truth is, I don't remember the moment, that exact moment, when I told him. I only recall that later, a week, maybe it was more, I saw Henry again, on the street. It was another college town that we were in then, and there was something going on, there was always something going on at that time, everybody was angry, there were marches and demonstrations, floods of students on the street, and in the midst of all that—the shouting and the music, drums and chants and the roiling crowd—I saw Henry, tall, his head above the others. His yellow hair, his blue coat, his amber eyes. I realize I couldn't have seen their color from that far away, but I remember it this way. Mixed with other memories, I suppose, of when we were together, those three years, which seemed significant then, but now it's a trifle, fleeting, compared with the almost forty that I've since been with John.

I turned away. I saw Henry see me, I saw the smile, his mouth opened and he was about to speak, but I pretended not to see and I turned away, ducked off, fled, because already there was John. I skittered through the crowd, small, I slipped away and didn't stop, didn't listen to hear Henry calling to me, I didn't look back. John was there, waiting for me in the bar, and he gathered me in, his smile, his arm around me. He didn't miss a beat. Just pulled me close and went on talking to the others who were with him, watching this, watching me, listening to him and whatever it was that he had to say. Which could have been anything.

I've burned the second note in the kitchen sink, the way you see people do in films. Then I ran water. Turned on the disposal. Washed my hands. I won't say anything. I won't do anything. I am the ground. I am the rock.

This afternoon, as I was cutting back the roses and bundling them in burlap, I thought of Henry again. I saw my own hands, and they seemed to belong to someone else. I touched my face, pulled at my hair. I watched the birds in the tree take off and swoop across the sky, the woods, the lawn. I felt Henry there.

Now it's dark, and I'm here in the house alone. John has called to tell me he won't be home for dinner—a meeting, he said, something, I don't know, they had to talk about the student-something, and he said he'd be late, don't worry about him, don't wait up.

Alone then, in our beautiful big house, more space, more of everything, than the two of us together need. The rugs. The crystal. The wide stairs. Emily was here earlier, cleaning, but by now she's gone and there's a fire and candles and music and a glass of wine. The bottle on the table, within easy reach. A cascade of roses, the last of them. And an old photograph album, with shots of me as a child, a girl, a young woman, all from the years that came before I knew John. I study my face and think I see there the shadow of myself as I am now, lurking behind the features of my face as I was then. As if it's a promise that I didn't know I'd made.

I've begun to regret burning the note, destroying it. I'd like to look at it again. The stab of those words felt good somehow. I've always known, of course, but this is different. Someone else knows now too. And having told me, that person also knows that I know, and whoever it is, they are waiting, watching to see what I will do.

The television is a secret vice. I turn it on when John's not here, which is more and more often lately. At first it was just sound, to keep me company. In the middle of the morning on a crushing late summer day when the sunshine and the blue sky and the cicadas and the whole damned fecundity of it all made me feel like a tiny little ball rattling around inside an empty box, so I went into the den, where it was dark and cool and the shades were pulled, the lights were off and I turned on the TV. A beer that time. Then it was a bottle of wine. Finally it is vodka, cold and clear, a knife that can be counted on to cut through the gauze, the mist, the fog. The crap.

I sit in John's leather chair before the big screen. This is where he watches films or listens to music. All a part of the process he has said, famously, in interviews and on other screens with other people watching, rapt. John—everybody loves him. He is very much admired. His light falls far.

His collection is impressive. And the sound system is excellent. But I ignore all that and change the input mode to television—always careful to change it back so he won't know. Not that he would be angry. He would just take it as another dent in my fender. A chip in my china. I smile at this, my teeth on the rim of my glass.

Channel 7. 11:00 a.m. Dr. Valentine's face fills the screen, her eyes brimming, her lips pressed, a crease of pain on her beautiful clear brow. A close-up, just before the camera pulls back to reveal the set, the audience, the couple on the sofa opposite, sitting close, and an old woman limp in a wheelchair, chin on her chest. The audience, applauding madly. Whistles and hoots and Dr. Valentine with a hand up to hush them before she turns to the couple and asks them, for what seems to be at least the second time: What will you do? The man stands. He takes one step and then he's on his knees before the old woman. He peers into her face, then turns to Dr. Valentine and smiling, tearfully, he murmurs something, too softly for the microphones to pick up. Dr. Valentine tilts her head. Cups her ear. He speaks up. She still can't hear him. He pulls himself to his feet, turns to look at me. His face, a grimace. The right thing, he says. I'll do the right thing. And the audience goes wild.

Last night John sat across from me at dinner, smiling as if the world were whole, and said it would just be a short trip, he'd only be gone for the weekend. I could come along, but why would I want to do that? He'd be in meetings the whole time, and the city was not an interesting one, not this time. Brutal in winter anyway, frozen solid. I'd be stuck in the room, I'd be unhappy, I'd be better off at home, and didn't I agree? I could tell he was lying, of course. But I don't try to imagine anymore about what might be the real story. Probably he isn't going anywhere at all.

This morning the boy was here to plow the driveway after last night's snow. And John was in the kitchen, impatient. Ready to go out, but waiting for the plowing to be done. I was waiting, too, in my room at the other end of the house. My poems. My scrapbooks. My flowers, my chocolates, my books. Women's work. In a silk robe with more flowers. My hair piled up on my head in a way that has always felt glamorous to me. A cup of tea, steaming. And I wondered, what would Henry think? What would he say, to see me now— older, fatter, softer.

The truck out there, with its plow blade scraping at the asphalt. Drifts piling up on either side. The light post capped with snow. And John's footsteps coming to me from the far end of the house. I could hear him and then he was there, in the doorway. His hand on my back, breath in my ear, lips on my cheek.

Saying, You know where to reach me. Meaning, his cell phone. And, Enjoy your solitude, darling. The smell of his cologne. Hair. Skin. I did not move as he drew away. His footsteps receding. His bag already in the car, backing out, turning around, and then, the long drive. Taillights, exhaust, and he was gone.

My solitude folded down over me.

When we brought this dog home two years ago, I was glad to have it. Company, John said. Protection, I thought, but from what? A companion, Emily assumed, with my husband traveling and me alone in the house so much of the time. She comes in once a week to clean, but that isn't company, that's something else, and I stay away. I'm a kept woman, I've joked, to friends and strangers both, but of course it's not a joke. They never are.

Small, black and white, a mop of curly hair, the kind of dog you see on television, in a family show, or on a commercial, a movie dog, a trick dog, an all-American dog, nipping at your heels. Curled up at the foot of your bed, following you from room to room. Lifting its head to look at you as if it knows something, then tearing through the house, barking, to the front door, because someone is there, leaving a package on the porch.

At church they talk about words and deeds and the difference between them. What we say and what we do. They've been horrified by what's been taking place at a truck stop out on the Interstate, not far from here. They know about it, and they talk about it, but what can anybody do? They showed photographs, but I looked away. And the woman in the next chair gave me a nudge. Come on, she said, it doesn't do any good to pretend it isn't there. So strident. Her hair a mess. Her fingernails chewed. I told John about this and he smiled. Why do you go there? he asked. To church, he meant. He shook his head. Lit the candles. Poured wine. Turned up the music. Smiled and reached for me. His lips at my ear, whispering: You're safe.

Little girls. Young women. Taken from their mothers or given away by their fathers or sold by who knows who.

I drove out there to see it for myself and then sat in the parking lot. But I saw nothing. The huge trucks, steaming, sighing, like large animals. Horses snuffling in their stalls. A woman and a girl in a red car near me, arguing. A man with a limp. The neon of the sign, glowing, for everyone to see.

I've put the package in the trash bin; I've buried it under the plastic bags of garbage that Emily left out for the collectors to take away. Maybe it's evidence, but it can't be proof.

What John said to me, in the beginning: This will be our arrangement. It has nothing to do with you. It's me. It's who I am. It changes nothing between us.

We are more modern than our friends, John said. We're not like other people.

And I'd loved that. My own rarity.

This house hums. Sometimes it sounds like voices in another room. Their conversations, their accusations, their announcements, their instructions, their questions, their judgments, their decrees.

Or whispers, mumbles, murmurs. The slurred mutterings of a drunk.

Or an announcer on the radio, on the television, volume low. I crane to catch what she's saying, what she's trying to tell me, but I can't quite make it out.

I used to go from room to room, trying to find her, but I don't bother with that anymore.

I've come to believe that there are many things not meant for me to know.

AMITY

Yes, I knew what was wrong. And I knew what had happened, and I knew my name, and I knew where I was, and I knew who you were, and I knew what you wanted from me too. I would have said so if I could. Not that I had anything to prove. Not that I wanted anything from you. Just to put you at ease, to let you know I was all right. The words were there but I couldn't get to them. They were trapped somewhere beyond me, and somehow they formed and floated, but when I tried to catch them with my tongue, they dissolved. I know what that must have looked like, me flopping my mouth open and shut like a landed fish. You would have liked to conk me on the head and be done with it, I knew that too. I could see it in your smirk. You'd have liked to give me a good kick. At least a good rattle—the way you used to shake and shake your dolls. You see, I was still there. No matter what it might have looked like to you.

What had happened to me was only a failure of body; it was not a problem of mind.

I was sitting in my chair, as always. I had been doing the crossword, as was my habit. Searching for words, even then. Eating mints for breakfast and maybe that was wrong, but I would have had the protein shake too—later, as instructed. I would have eaten my lunch—cleared my plate. I would have eaten my

It's Not About the Dog | 133

dinner—same. Waste not, want not—all that never changed. I am a good girl. I do what I'm told. I stuck to the schedule. Except: chocolate mint patties in the morning. My secret. And really: who cares?

The first thing: my pencil faltered. Then: my hand froze. The chocolate was melting in my mouth, and I licked it off my teeth, felt the dribble of it down my chin, thought to wipe it with the tissue crumpled in my other hand. Heard the finches at the feeder outside my window. And the sigh of the refrigerator. The knacker of the kitchen clock. The rustle of my fine silk robe.

It was just this: I couldn't move. There was a flutter to the side, where the shadows seemed to shift. Or no, it was more like a light had gone out, down the hall, in the bedroom, in the bathroom. At first I thought there'd been some sort of catastrophe. The kind you read about in books. A bomb, say. An invasion. Tsunami. Earthquake. Tornado. But the window was bright. The leaves green. Sky blue and not a cloud.

And then it all collapsed. An implosion, like. The world folded in around me. I folded in upon myself.

How long? I don't know. I heard you tell the doctor: It could have been days. Before you called. Before you came. Before you found me there.

Amity. My daughter. St. Anne's Hospital. 7th Floor. ICU. Mary. A stroke. A blood clot on a mission of erasure from my leg up into my brain.

They've moved me to a private room, because I have the money to pay to be here on my own, no slab of flesh snoring and rotting and passing gas in the next bed. I know I have Ham to thank for this, as for everything else that's ever in my lifetime been mine. I'm grateful, too, that he's not here to see me now.

The doctor has explained that if I feel emotionally

overwhelmed, that's due to the situation in my noggin. He spoke slowly, brought his face close to mine. Whiskers on his chin; onions for lunch.

"A stroke is a strangulation of an area of the brain due to a lack of oxygen caused by a blockage, hemorrhage, or embolism. Symptoms and aftereffects of a stroke will vary depending on where the stroke occurs. Movement and sensation for one side of the body is controlled by the opposite side of the brain."

I'm not a foreigner, I wanted to say, and I'm not deaf, I wanted to shout, but I couldn't do either, and that's what's what. My tongue is tied. He's explained that part to me too, and when you showed up I had to listen to it all over again. You brought flowers and chocolates, books, a crossword, and Brattles too, because that's not only allowed, it's encouraged. He leaped up onto the bed and licked my face and panted and barked. His small paws tramped all over me. I held him in my one good arm, and you beamed, happy to have provided such a thing, then pulled open the curtains to bring in the sunlight too. Vased the flowers, placed the books, unwrapped the chocolates, turned off the TV.

"See, Mom," you said. "Just like home."

Amity. Your soft hands and doughy face. Your blunt-cut hair, dry as straw. A cow, I thought, looking at you. And was ashamed.

Now the burden shows itself, because any conversation can only be one-sided. At first I struggled to respond, but I now I've given up and settled back to let you do all the work, for once.

Amity. You were the little girl in the calico dress I made for you myself. Not because I had to but just because I could. You were the silent one then, as a child, wide-eyed and reserved, never the first to laugh or have anything to say. Instead you stood back and you faded.

Sometimes it was easy to forget you were there. The three of us, you and Ham and me, we were a quiet little family. Over dinner, for example. Eating on the good china at my mother's lovely table. Our small house was just big enough for us, with a sunny yard and a garden for Ham to tend and an extra room for me and my sewing. I am only remembering the good parts, no doubt. There must have been dark days too, but if there were, I can't recall them anymore.

Now that silence seems an obstacle. You do your best to fill the gap of me with your own voice. Mostly complaints, though you wouldn't like to know that. You're in a pickle yourself, after all, with your own kids gone, the last one off to college, and your own house—much bigger and noisier and messier than mine ever was—looming over you, with all its particular requirements and care. Now you're telling me: Frank has left you too. You dab a tear and cock your head, smiling wistfully, then pull a wad of knitting from your bag. Busy hands, I know.

And so that's how we are then. Me in my bed, clutching Brattles, who's sound asleep. Your needles flashing. The flowers wafting in the breeze from the overhead fan.

And neither of us with anything more to say.

The next time you come to visit, I am that much better. Sitting in a chair, so improved I've expected you to be shocked by the nice surprise of at least having the worry for me lifted from what you like to call your full plate. They've washed my hair and combed it, even clipped a little pin here at the side to pull it back from my face, so I am no longer the witch I've recently been. Though the pin pinches, I've chosen to consider that a good thing, a feeling I can feel, a reminder to myself that I am here. My hands are folded in my lap, positioned so you wouldn't know one of them is dead weight, entirely useless to me anymore. My bad leg in a brace. The struggle of dressing minimized by simple clothes, and ample. Plenty of room in these pants, for all of me and then some. Even shoes with Velcro straps—though not very dainty, at least they're new. Bright white. Athletic shoes. As if.

The flowers on the tables and the windowsill pile up. Here is a carafe of fresh water. And books, useless to me anymore. Magazines, the same. But I refuse the television and sit instead in my own silence, admiring the sparkle of the parking lot below and the blooming trees beyond.

This time you haven't brought the dog along. Your explanation for why not—even the nurses have been looking forward to seeing him—reveals to me the truth. You've got rid of him. My Brattles. When I make a fuss—moaning and gawping and struggling to stand— you admit the truth, then do your best to bury it in another lie.

You've passed him on to a good family. "It's for the best," you say. "He has a great home now." You can't be home all the time with him, the way that I've been. He was lonely—which I take to mean he's ruined something, one of your expensive shoes maybe, your furniture, your rug. I close my eyes against the vision of the violence of what I can guess was your response. You would have killed him, I think, and I check your hands for bite marks, scratches, but am relieved to find no such thing—just your perfect manicure instead.

Still, you overdo it so much, simpering, kneeling by my chair, I am afraid you might be about to put your head in my lap. Asking for forgiveness, telling me how hard this is for you.

"You're not the only one who suffers," you say. And the nurse, in the doorway, with a tray, meets my look. Pauses. Then creeps away.

This morning you've come to visit me again, with more flowers and the chocolate mints you know I like. Bossing the nurses around and making things nice in my room. Offering me a pillow you've bought, with some oriental silk design. It's pretty maybe, but not my style, and I wonder what you were thinking. Still, I hold it in my lap and the weight of it feels good. The fabric is pleasant to the touch. I'm fingering it at the corner, taking comfort the way I used to take it from the satin trim of a blanket when I was a child. Or the silky feel of Brattles's ear lately. No more news on that front. I'm left to picture him happily romping in the green grass of someone else's enormous front yard. Yapping after squirrels. Barking at the sky.

You sit across from me. Me in my chair. Feet on the flaps. My leg in its brace and the clumsy shoes on my feet, sized up a notch to accommodate the swelling. The PT has me lifting my arms up over my head, but I don't like to do it, and I resist and refuse until, with your negative reinforcement added in, he gives up and lets me be. I'm grateful to you for that. Big bossy girl, you've always been one to have your way.

Other news: you've lost your job. Or maybe you quit. It's not clear and I can't ask and it doesn't matter. I'm going to guess you were fired, because it wouldn't surprise me and it wouldn't be the first time either. "A shit job anyway," you say, and you can see me flinch at the word but you don't care. Anything for a reaction. Another quirk: wanting a response, doesn't matter if it's good or bad.

You're telling me you've hired a cleaning service to take care of my apartment. Keep it in order, ready for when they let me go back. You've used your power of attorney to write the checks to pay the bills, and you've been sorting through things too, while you're at it. I don't want to think about what that means—you with your hands all over everything, judging me.

You're the kind of person who will always turn a conversation, any conversation, doesn't matter what it is—politics, religion, the weather, the price of corn—to yourself, to some anecdote in which you are the star. "Oh, that reminds me," you say. Or, "It's just like the time I…" Or, "I did that once myself." Or, "Well, for me, it's…" Turning a conversation into a monologue. A dialogue into a diatribe. I wonder if that's my fault. I am your mother, after all. Ham and I let you have center stage too often, maybe. We listened too closely to you, paid too much attention, let you think it mattered who you were and what you had to say.

Ham always said we should have had another child.

But now that I can't talk, it's all lots easier for you. You don't have to work to turn the conversation around to face and mirror you. You can start right there, gazing at your own reflection, with me right here, a captive audience for it all.

When a person can't talk, people will react in different ways. Some run off as fast as they can. They bring a gift, pay a visit, but I can see they're anxious to get away, and sometimes it can be amusing to try to prolong their discomfort. Keep them captive and watch them squirm.

Others assume if I can't talk, then I must not be able to hear either. They shout at me and mistake my wince for anguish, my scowl for grief.

Then there are the ones who try to do my talking for me. Filling in the empty spaces with what they think I would be saying if I only could. These folks I can listen to forever. I never want this one to leave, and I'm saddened when she does—she must, she has other things to do—because I always feel she's taken some vital bit of me along with her when she goes.

You, however, are different. You just talk and talk, creating a drone of information that fills the room like the hum of the refrigerator or the whirring of the fan. Pretty soon I don't even hear it anymore and only miss it when it suddenly stops.

I am beginning to unfold. A door cracks open. A window lifts. The power will come back in an instant, dark to light, but this is different, a slow seepage of forgotten words. Paradigm. Incubate. Calipers. Penchant. Relegate. They have no context, they're just sounds that float up like bubbled captions. I move my jaw, lick my lips, prepare to speak. Soon. I can feel it coming. Anon.

You whirl in with a bag of bagels, coffee, oranges. The unsaid is like a boulder on my chest, making it hard for me to breathe.

Imperturbable.

A fluff of cream cheese adheres to your lip, and I gesture but you don't understand, and so I watch it float there as you rattle on and on, filling up all the empty spaces with the sound of your own voice. As a child you made noise just to prove that you were there, you were real. Constantly calling out "Hello!" into the void.

Restitution.
Permeable.
Valence.

The coffee burns and I yelp, which makes you smile.

Fracking.
Querulous.
Eventual.

You've decided not to bother looking for another job. Not right away anyway. You're old enough to retire, plenty of women stop working at your age. Plenty of women your age have never worked at all. You've also put your house up for sale, at a good price because you want to get it done, get it gone and off your hands, because, you reason, there could be another real estate crash, and even if this isn't the best time to sell, it might also not yet be the worst, and you don't want to take chances. Explaining all of this to me as we sit in my room. With the flowers you've brought—always flowers—so many now a person might think, by the look of them all, that someone's died. The nurses twinkle at me: "Somebody loves you, dear!"

Meanwhile you've moved into my apartment. You've cleaned it up, you say. Taken out the carpet—pee-stained—odorous—"How did you stand the stench?"—and replaced it with wood floors. Upgraded the kitchen. "That old refrigerator! Practically an icebox!" Cleaned the cupboards. "I've sorted things for you, Mother. I've simplified." Installed rails in the bathroom. Arranged the furniture so there is plenty of space for the wheelchair to move around. You had to get rid of a few things to make that work. Set up a hospital bed in the little room that used to be my office. It will be better for me, you insist. A better view, too, of the lawn and the street below. I'll be able to see what people are doing out there. How life goes on.

You've taken my bedroom for yourself.

You'll take care of me, you say.

The words flood in now:

Preemptive.
Comfort.
Possession.
Caretaker.

Undulate.
Sisyphian.
Objet d'art.
Longevity.

I maintain my silence anyway.

When I get home, I see all that you've done to make this a place for us to live together. For as long as it takes.

"It's only temporary," you say.

I know I should be grateful. I should say "Thank you," but I don't. Not because I can't. Because I won't.

I bite my tongue and give it to the cat.

THE WOODSMAN

It's a famous scene in certain circles. The girl is on the ground, and she's lying there with her knees up, but you can't really tell what's happening until the camera pulls away and then you see the back of his head as he closes over her. His hair is glossy; her skin shines in the moonlight. The forest trees loom over them. There's a sound and her eyes open. A close-up on her face and you can't tell whether what you're looking at is an expression of ecstasy or terror. Then it's all just shadows and screams. Cut to the bright sun, grass so green it seems painted, and a thick pool of red so dark it's black. A sound of flies. Pan up to the trees now, to see her trussed and dripping like an exsanguinated pig.

We used to throw a little party on Wednesday nights after prayer group, which Elsie led in the chapel where the light at that time of day spilled in through the stained glass and gave the faces of my friends a glow that was like what happens in summer at sunset just before the fireflies come out. Seeing it, you had to think that what we did was true and right and good and not the waste of time some people would rather have believed it was.

After prayer it was potluck in the social hall, with Alice's peas and onions and my mac and cheese and the salads and rolls and tuna casseroles that were the usual fare. Mary Beth's Hamburger Helper and Fran's Tater

Tot Pie. All set up and the tables out and sometimes, this time, Jeff Prince was up there with his guitar and his brother Travis on the piano too. The sound of us echoed in the room: Where two or three are gathered, and all like that. It was a joyous thing, even with the sick and the hobbled, the oldsters nodding over their plates and old Margaret in her wheelchair dozing through her meal. Although it wasn't exactly open to the public, sometimes someone from outside would show up and we were happy to feed them too, of course. We would not say no, not if he came to us and he was hungry, even in his old sweater and his greasy hair and his torn pants and broken shoes, even if he looked like a bum and better off in line at the food pantry than there at our buffet. His beard coming in dark on his cheeks. And blond hair cut to stand up straight on his head. But when he smiled, his teeth were perfect, white and clean and straight—the grin of a salesman at your door and blue eyes bright and quick to catch you in them, sudden, like a fish hook. He'd draw you in and you'd be thinking there might even be something holy about that man among us. This might be a test. Don't you dare turn him away.

At the same time, there was something familiar there in his eyes, and everyone else was nodding and smiling too hard and talking too loudly or too softly, moving toward him or away from him, depending on the depth of their faith or their acceptance of the challenge. Marie Smith—with her hair all done up and jewelry dangling, hips stuffed into the stretch of turquoise pants and her skin orange with that fake tanning cream, lips puckered pink and lashes batting black gunk—she moved close and drawled a question at him, but I could have told her it wasn't Jesus and it wasn't just a bum either that we were looking at. It came to me when I saw him turn and the way he towered over her, plate in hand and chewing on a sandwich, it was Nick Finn, come back from the dead past.

His father had been my father's friend and might also have been my mother's lover too. Just that one time at least and likely more than that. Maybe for months. Possibly for years. They sheltered in each other because my father and his mother had been going at it already. They had a thing that everybody knew about but nobody wanted to say they'd seen and no one said a thing about the thing, except my mother when she found out, the last to know and isn't it always so? She raged and wept and threw things, broke things, drove too fast and drank too much and endangered herself and her children, too, including me, until one close call too many brought her to her senses and caused her to calm down. At which point she thanked the Lord for sparing her and begged forgiveness and took another tack.

Sarah Bernhardt, my father called her, for the dramatics, for the scenes, but it was Mrs. Finn herself who was the real actress, star of our community theater, famous for her place up there on that small stage. My father sat in the audience, laughing along with the rest of them, his eyes shining. He was in love with her, that was clear, but so was everybody. At least that's how my mother told it, all those years later, when she was confined to her apartment, which was filled with extra oxygen from the compressor because she suffered from emphysema on account of all the cigarettes. They had been glamorous at first and powerful in a way too. The tobacco companies advertised especially to women at that time, telling them that they were free and equal and could smoke like a man and think like a man and work like a man and vote like a man if that was what they wanted. And die too, it turned out, because human lungs are all the same, after all. Still those campaigns got to my mother—small-town girl with lovely legs—and it was a long time, many years, too many years, before she finally gave it up, the glamor and the beauty and the smoking, too, because the beauty had left her and the glamor had become a joke in stretch pants and sensible shoes and the smoking had turned into a cough she couldn't shake.

When we were teens, I introduced Nick to a friend and it was a good match. They hit it off and traded rings and rode around in his car and danced at the parties and kissed in the dark and groped in the shadows, got married, and settled down, but when she ended it—I don't know why—he wouldn't have it. He became abrasive then and unpredictable. He said she was cracked, but he couldn't let her go. He followed her around and tried to have her committed, and none of us knew which one of them was the liar, who was the nut, who was to blame. Pretty soon both of them disappeared.

As for Nick's father, he'd been a fishermen like my dad was too. There was an accident, where he drowned in the river when their canoe capsized. My father, who was a smaller man and a better swimmer and who held onto a tree branch until help arrived or he pulled himself to safety, I don't remember which—he survived. The river was high that summer, after a deluge in late spring. They shouldn't have been out there. Mr. Finn's body was found several miles downstream. And so on: bashed and battered. Identified by the family, maybe Nick himself, cremated at the local mortuary. Ashes scattered on the river. Fish food. Tit for tat, I guess. A tragedy wasn't it? No, it was not. Just an accident, simple like that.

When Nick showed up, it was that many years later and by then his mother was gone too. He was all alone, it looked like, and though I paused to feel sorry for him, I also had to acknowledge the clear contempt he had for my sympathy. No hard feelings from before though. His smile was warm and he said my name, fully recognized me, knew me, as if nothing had happened and no time had passed. He didn't mention his clothes or say what he was doing there at the church that night. That was obvious, wasn't it? He was eating supper with us. It was a place of God, see. Everybody welcome and all that.

He wanted to say hello to my mom and so I invited him to come by to visit, and when I told her, she was pleased and anxious for him to appear. He'd cleaned himself up in the meantime, to show that not much had changed. Still handsome. Still strong. His face had weathered a little, and his hands had hardened. Still, he cleaned up good and sat on her porch in a bright yellow shirt and neatly pressed jeans, smiling at her every word, sipping the watered-down lemonade she served him, refusing her offer of a real drink. No ring on his finger, by the way.

She doted on him and he began to visit her regularly then. Sundays after church, which he also attended. Keeping to himself in a pew at the back, slipping in late and out early, which was his privilege, of course, and which also caused a wave of gossip, a titter among the hens, who noticed and were intrigued.

It pleased my mom to hear that he'd lost his mother to diabetes. Mrs. Finn had lost one leg first and then the other. Had gone to fat too. Big, bloated, and bald in a wheelchair, until she went into a coma and then the rest was up to Nick. My mother liked to tell him he'd made a courageous choice, that it was an act of generosity, an act of love, while to her it was a kind of triumph. Like, there she was, still among the living, and somehow in the end, after all that went on, through pure tenacity, she'd won.

She was in self-preservation mode then. Keeping herself alive, not healthy, not strong, just alive. One day after the other, the same routine. Here I am. Breakfast, lunch, dinner. A schedule built around mealtimes, with small extra activities in between. Naps, sleep, cards, television, crossword puzzles, a phone call, a book. The hours whiled away. The days passing. Seasons turning. The apartment filled with cool clear air from the compressor and every excursion—to the doctor or the grocery store, a visit with an old friend, dinner out, a holiday—was a trauma that had her groping for home.

She would live forever this way, she thought, though of course she didn't. She was wrong about that, as are we all. Death came calling for her too, just like anybody else. Pneumonia. That was all it took. One winter when the snow was deep and she was snug and, she thought, safe. Maybe it was Nick Finn himself, bearing flowers and fruits, candy and cake, come to see her after church. To fill the apartment with his presence. She blushed and giggled, tittered, smiled, her voice deepened and she glittered, she twinkled at him like a star. Even as he sat there, smiling, filling the air with his stink. Poisoning it with his germs.

The blame came later. I thought it, but didn't believe it, not at first. We were friends, after all, and I saw him sometimes. We talked on the phone now and then. Late at night, he would call. He was traveling, he said. He had a lot to do, a lot on his plate, the prime of his life and such. But also he was ragged and he didn't seem to have a home, not that I ever saw anyway, though I told him he ought to have me over sometime. For dinner or drinks, and he looked at me and smiled and shook his head in that way people do when they think you're joking and they think it's funny but maybe it's not, except it would be easier for them if they could see that you were just kidding when you said that outrageous thing and so that's how they'd prefer to take it. And fondly so, appreciative of your crazy humor, like.

After that it was as if we shared the secret of his destitution, his homelessness, and his dereliction, something about him we both knew but never mentioned, as if we'd already talked it out and come to some conclusion, though we hadn't done that, and so it was all just pretend anyway.

Which opened the door to make-believe and I walked in and made that place my home, with Nick Finn right there in it, front and center. That thinking carried me through a lot and for a long time. My pretend boyfriend. I had moved into my mother's apartment by then, and Nick came to see me every once in a while, just like he'd come to see her. I was teaching and spending plenty of time at the church then too, offering up prayers for the dying and the sick, not leaving much room for myself in there, because I considered it unnecessary. I had everything I needed, I thought, and then some. When I look back now at what all that must have looked like, I ache through and through, with shame.

Last time I saw Nick was at the diner down on Farmington Way, out by the fairgrounds, where Mitch Hanley took an old railroad car and made it into a restaurant that's been in the papers and on TV, famous like that. Nick was there in a booth when I came in, which I did with some regularity due to the prices and the burgers I could not get enough of. Feeling good because I'd had my hair done just that morning and a new dress that fell nicely and covered up some of the extra pounds that had accumulated here and there. At least that kept my face pretty, I told myself. Cheeks full and shining skin. And we all have to eat.

He was sitting at a booth by the window at the back, near the door that led out to the kitchen, which was an add-on to the car. Just the smell of the place was enough to bring me peace. Early in the afternoon, so the dinner crowd hadn't turned up yet, which suited me. I preferred to eat alone and unobserved at the counter on a stool, plenty of room on all sides, but there was Nick and he saw me before I saw him, and he called me over and invited me to join him. I couldn't see any way out, so there I was, dream and nightmare come true both at the same time. He was as shabby as ever, in some torn shirt with stains on it and a tie he'd loosened, but it wasn't a nice one. His hair was straw on his head and he had some extra wrinkles added in, to give his face a little character. He was starting to look truly weathered, like an old porch post somebody forgot to paint.

I had a salad for myself, while he was finishing up pie and coffee. On the road, he said and about to go pick up a new car at the Ford place across town. I found this hard to believe. I tried to hide my doubt, but already by then it had occurred to me that maybe his filth had had something to do with my mother's illness and consequent death, so I was looking at him in a new light. This was not the pretend boyfriend. Those two had split off and gone their separate ways, so who was this one when the other one was waiting for me and ready to show up whenever I needed him, whenever I called. I came right out with it, my doubt. Mouth full of spinach and the smell of the onions on that grill slapping my senses silly. Let the curtain part on the truth and my knowing of it, by not saying, "Oh, that's nice," but "How in the world can you afford a thing like that?" Expecting to stop him in his tracks that way. But he didn't miss a beat. Smiling like he could—and there was an inkling of the fantasy in it when he leaned closer with that gleam in eye and tooth to tell me in a low voice, like it was a secret something, just between us and anybody watching from a distance might have seen this and mistaken it for intimacy, his paw on my hand and spinach in my teeth—that he had written a bad check.

I pulled back. I told him not to do it. Lousy idea, Nick. He'd get in trouble. Go to jail even. But he said no and explained how he already had the cash in hand. Now all he had to do was go over and pick up that car. A Mustang, he said. Convertible. Cherry red. He wanted me to go with him, but I found a way to say no, probably not, I was otherwise engaged that evening, not letting on that it was with a figment of my imagination that only faintly reminded me of him.

I never saw him again, though I had my eye out for that cherry car and added it to the imagined life, right alongside the house and the kids and the man at the dinner table complimenting me on my cooking and then taking me in his arms.

My father had ideas about reality, physics, what was possible and what was not. Statistics, like, and contingencies, probabilities. He had a theory that sounded something like fate. The temperature of the water, the velocity of the flow, plus the direction of the wind. Factored in against the weight of two men and the buoyancy of a canoe. Plus, the sins of Mr. Finn.

But this was all a long time ago. Nick Finn is dead now. I heard about it at church, at the pancake breakfast on Easter morning, where I was watching over the kids, whose event it was. Teenagers flipping pancakes and pouring juice. Their bright smiles and eager faces. New dresses and pressed shirts. Shined shoes. Damp hair. Laughing in the kitchen, clattering pots and pans and plates and trays and me bustling in and out, working up a sweat. I took a breather when that first rush slowed.

"He is risen."

"He is risen indeed."

Two hens gossiping in the kitchen. I picked up on the name and sat up straight, listening, craning for more, past the laughter of the kids and all their noise, plus the music starting up in the sanctuary downstairs.

The proof was in the paper the next day. Nicholas Finn. A long illness. Author of novels I'd never heard of, which had inspired movies I'd never seen. Fancy that. With a young wife. A child. Houses and cars and property in places I've never been.

I've seen all those movies now. Some more than once. The one with the trussed girl, that's my favorite: *The Woodsman 3: Slaughter Me Softly.* It's still on TV every now and then. Late. Smattered with commercials. The most graphic of the sex scenes have been excised, but the bloodfest is still pretty much intact.

CAUGHT

~~~~~~

She fixes herself a drink and sits in front of the television, not watching the news but rather looking at the photograph in its frame. There Alan smiles to himself, unaware of the camera that's caught him.

She was standing outside, trying to get a shot of the garden to send to her sister, and she turned, saw a movement at the window. Alan had just come in from the pool and was dressing for dinner.

She slipped across the lawn toward the house. Her breath seized as it had when she was a shoplifting teen, so much wilder then than now. She thought she understood why this was—her mother's unrelenting disapproval fueling the fear and at the same time the thrill that comes from doing something so unnecessary and so wrong. She'd had money in her purse after all.

Caught, how would she explain?

She stood close to the open window, watching him. Fair hair, only just beginning to thin. Tanned hands working the buttons of his laundered shirt. Gold watch glinting on his wrist. And, that smile.

She raised the camera to her eye.

It wasn't until later, when she'd had the roll developed and was looking through her shots of the garden to choose which would most impress her sister, that she came upon this one of Alan, dressing for dinner, in the bedroom alone. At first she couldn't remember, when had she taken it? Where?

And what had he been thinking?

She didn't show it to him. She kept it a secret from him. Something private of her own that she looked at, even when he was right there with her, in the same room.

Knowing she'd already lost him.

And now that he's gone, she's had it framed.

"It's Not About The Dog" first appeared in *Guernica Magazine*.

"Witness" first appeared in *Amarillo Bay*.

"What We Forget" first appeared in *Juked*.

"Dear Mr. Fantasy" first appeared in *Necessary Fiction*.

"Phipp" first appeared in *The Coe Review*.

"Just So" first appeared in *Folio*.

"The Most Terrible Thing" first appeared in *Word Riot*.

"Mouse Wars" first appeared in *Verdad Magazine*.

"All The Time" will appear in Issue 12 of *Monday Night*.

"The View From Here" first appeared in *Folly Magazine* and *Schuylkill Valley Journal*.

"The Lost Art of Listening" first appeared in *Blue Lake Review*.

"Dawn" first appeared in *Permafrost Magazine*.

"What She Didn't Do" first appeared in *Conte*.

"The Beginning Of The End Of All That" first appeared in *The Adirondack Review*.

"Amity" first appeared in *Grey Sparrow Journal*.

ALSO BY SUSAN TAYLOR CHEHAK

The Minor Apocalypse of Meena Krejci

"It begins like a storm—with that pensive heavy stillness of dead air pressing in, with a soft rustle of the wind just barely stirring in the trees, a bruising over of the summer sky, a somber gray and yellow horizon glittery with lightning, bloated full of thunder, swept by sheets of rain—it begins when old man Krejci bumps his head. And then—like that same storm spent, blown past to leave the ground and the air around feeling new and fresh and washed crisp clean—the next morning when Meena peeks into her father's sun-spilled bedroom to find that he has not moved, but is still lying on the bed with his head flat back on the pillow, in just exactly the same way she left him there eight hours before, everything will be changed…"

It begins when Meena Krejci, not sure what to do and fearing she'll be blamed for the injuries that have caused her father's death, panics and takes flight, driving west across Nebraska and into Colorado, where she encounters an apocalypse-predicting madman, his captive sister—the troubled young woman in whose release Meena will create a violent version of rebirth for herself—and a bear. Told through alternating narratives—a portrayal of the last few days of Meena's life and an account of the events in the past that have brought her to where she is now—this is the story of a woman running away from home for the first time and the strong, nearly universal desire to shed one's identity to become somebody else.

The Great Disappointment, A Confession

"[Chehak's] ambitiously imaginative novel questions the very nature of reality... [a] diverting exploration of metaphysical concepts. Winsome and smartly playful." —Kirkus Reviews

Rampage

"Chehak's darkly evocative Midwestern gothic is a stunning exploration of love, lust, greed, envy, innocence, murder, and obsession. Unforgettable characters, a grim and riveting plot, and darkly lyrical prose add up to great reading." —*Booklist*

Smithereens

"Vivid [and] intense SMITHEREENS has brooding, ominous atmosphere, sexual awakening, loss of innocence, murder. It could be described as a gothic coming-of-age novel, but it's far too good to lend itself to any label. Susan Taylor Chehak is a meticulous writer, an evocative stylist whose mastery is evident on every page." —*The Boston Globe*

Dancing on Glass

"A deeply chilling, disturbing, beautifully written novel. Shocking, stunningly written Faulkner himself would have admired and respected [DANCING ON GLASS]. Its events should linger in the reader's mind long after it has been read." —*Los Angeles Daily News*

Harmony

"One of those novels that returns to haunt you long after it's been replaced on the shelf." —*The Cleveland Plain Dealer*

The Story of Annie D.

"Absolutely stunning. Reads with the force and generational sweep of some ancient rural myth. Like the author, Annie D. is such a mesmerizing storyteller that you can almost feel the fire at your back." —*The New York Times Book Review*

ABOUT SUSAN TAYLOR CHEHAK

Susan Taylor Chehak is a graduate of the University of Iowa Writers' Workshop and the author of several novels, including *Smithereens*, *The Story of Annie D.*, and *Harmony*. Her short stories have appeared in Folio, Coe Review, Guernica Magazine, and The Adirondack Review, among other places. Susan has taught fiction writing in the low residency MFA program at Antioch University, Los Angeles, the UCLA Extension Writers' Program, the University of Southern California, and the Summer Writing Festival at the University of Iowa. She grew up in Cedar Rapids, Iowa, spent many years in Los Angeles, lives occasionally in Toronto, and at present calls Colorado her home.

Website: www.susantaylorchehak.com
Twitter: http://twitter.com/stchehak
Facebook: www.facebook.com/stchehak
Blog: www.tumblr.com/blog/susantaylorchehak

Find more good books at

Foreverland Press

www.foreverlandpress.com